Buzzed on Bacchus

D1518408

Mona Ventress

Blurb

The bathroom door leads to a narrow hall on a downward incline and doubles back on itself before ending in a second, matching door. A pulsing rhythm vibrates through the thick wood, so strong it bounces inside the frame. I can't hear anything else but knowing there's a Bacchanalia on the other side has my skin crawling under the weight of all the bodies waiting, ready to fall like an avalanche on my head. My burst of bravado vanishes, and anxiety blooms in their absence. I'm frozen, unable to take another step forward or even risk opening the door.

I take a deep breath and push it down. *I thought we were done with this, but for the last time: This is your chance to be different, Delilah. You're ready for this, you deserve this, and you can go home at any time.*

My hand quivers as I reach up and I have to grab the door handle just to make it stop. The metal feels wrong in my hands. Alien. I know it's just my panic, telling me to run and hide, and for once in my life, I don't want to listen. That story always has the same ending; me alone, without anyone to touch or be beside. I starve for affection. Crave attention.

I stare at the wood for a long moment. Then I turn the handle, pull it open, and throw all caution to the wind.

Content Warning

Greetings and Salutations my darling Moaners, and thank you for joining me as I chronicle Delilah's journey as a lover to the gods and other mythological beings. That said, let this serve as a warning: The beings and situations you will encounter on this journey aren't always pleasant, and can sometimes contain themes of violence, death, religion, substance abuse, misogyny, sexual assault, and other traumatizing situations that may be uncomfortable or triggering. Please, do not risk traumatizing (or even retraumatizing) yourself through exposure to these scenes. If you wish to read Delilah's story, but want to avoid these themes, please visit continue reading, to get a brief summary of the chapter(s) to avoid when reading.

Also, if you're easily offended by strangely shaped dongs, heteroeroticsm, homoeroticism, orgies with beings of various shapes, sizes, and animalistic design, and women with healthy sexual appetites who have multiple partners, then I suggest you return to the land of MC and billionaire bad boy erotica where it is much, much safer.

In Buzzed on Bacchus, there are scenes featuring substance abuse, specifically alcohol consumption, to the point of blacking out, which can be symptomatic of alcohol poisoning. If this is something you have a traumatic relationship with, then we recommend skipping the end of Chapter Five, Chapter Six, and the last four pages of Chapter Twelve.

Also, if you or someone you know is struggling with alcohol abuse, please contact the Substance Abuse and Mental Health Adminstration at 1-800-662-4357, or at https://www.samhsa.gov, to find local counseling, and remember to treat them (or even yourself) with the compassion and understanding they deserve, as substance abuse IS a mental health issue.

Summary:

At the end of Chapter Five, Delilah is pressured to drink some of Bacchus' wine under the threat of violence from his three Maenads. The wine is sweet and potent, and Delilah finds herself quickly intoxicated, to the point where she mouths off at the Maenads for being rude. Alyxs, the octopus-woman, seems to take Delilah's comments personally, and starts to attack, when the spotlight shines on them both, and Bacchus is beckoning Delilah forward.

In Chapter Six, Bacchus explains Delilah's punishment for breaking a cardinal rule in Nimble: Orgasms must be shared with a friend. As he shares how she will be co-starring in a play called *Temptress Punished* with not only him, but a third participant, Delilah drinks to calm her raging insecurities, to the point where she weaves back and forth and slurs her words, to the point where she's disrupting the show. Alyxs rudely suggests putting her into the shower to get rid of the dog smell, but Bacchus does it anyway, telling her it will give him time to pick the third and sober her up.

In the last four pages of Chapter Twelve, Delilah wonders when this will end, exhausted from multiple orgasms the alcohol coursing through her blood. She starts to fade, only to be woken up by Bacchani eating her out. She tries to get him to stop, body too sensitive from Luci's ministrations, but he ignores her. In retaliation, she sucks at the folds of flesh poking through the cock cage Alyxs put on him earlier. The pain is intense enough that he stops, but a strange taste explodes in Delilah's mouth, the tart slightly sour flavor reminiscent of the wine, and she realizes it's a more potent version of it, being produced by his dick. The strength hits her like a ton of bricks and the night fades to a blur after that, a whirlwind of sexual acts being performed on the other until she finally passes out.

Acknowledgements

There are so many people working tirelessly behind the scene that it never seems like there is enough space to acknowledge everyone. First, I gotta give it up to my buddy JJ. Without your tireless help, I never would've gotten moved in and settled to get this ready for publication in time. Also, Jami, whose observations as a beta reader helped me infinitely improve the story contained within these pages, and to Leah, my editor, for their infinite patience at how last-minute I got Jami's edits back to them. I promise I'll be faster in the future, but until then, I'm glad I've got you. Lastly, to Suzi, for whom the struggle has been unreal lately; you have been the best support network for me since I got back. Now it's my turn, bitch.

Manager: Suzann Addison
wordsmith.industries.llc@gmail.com

Editor: Leah Kist
leahkist@gmail.com

Beta Readers:
Jami Archer
Finn
Veronica Gonzales
Lashandra G.
J. Sánchez-Frost *seniastardust@gmail.com*
Robyn Latice *rlaticea@gmail.com*
Samantha Bartlett *sam.bartlett652@gmail.com*
Vanessa Thomas, M.Ed. *overthemoonproofreading.com*
Cover art: Em Gowan *emgowan.illustration@gmail.com*

Formatting: KT Ireland *wordsmithktireland@gmail.com*

Dedication

To Tim Curry: Your earlier work on Legend and Rocky Horror Picture Show inspired lots of what follows (as well as a few of my childhood masturbatory fantasies).

Also, for all those topping from the bottom: Without you we'd never know how to do anything right.

Table of Contents

Chapter One

"But I was hoping to stay with you. I mean… we barely had any time together! This can't possibly be it." I gaze at the Egyptian god of death, hoping my plea will change his mind.

Anubis meets my eyes, his glowing scarlet gaze revealing nothing. "I have upheld the terms of my contract. To keep you any longer, or for any additional pleasures, would bring the others crashing through my door, ready for war. While you are certainly worth fighting for, Delilah, I do not have the strength that the others do."

My heart aches for him and I reach out, wanting to reassure him with my touch, but he steps out of reach. "I thank you for your kindness, Delilah, but it's best if we don't."

I retract my hand and nod as if I understand, but

his rejection – however understandable – still stings.

"I'll send you ahead to the next suitor," he continues, seemingly oblivious. "I assure you; they will see to your needs." It takes a moment to register what he's saying, but when I do, I look up at him, ready to object, only to find his hand in the air and mouth moving. "Good luck on your adventure, dear one. Try to remember what I've said."

He waves and the world goes black. Everything disappears except gravity, but instead of dragging me down, it pulls me up. Rising, I tumble on all axes with the grace of a book flung into the air. Vertigo assails my senses, making the urge to vomit come and go like a vicious merry-go-round. I scream, but the sound is lost to the wind whistling past indicating high velocity. In my mind, I see myself plummeting toward the surface of the earth – a humanoid meteorite punching through the earth's crust – and cradling my head with my arms in a pathetic attempt at self-preservation.

It stops as suddenly as it began, the wind and the strange forces pulling me disappearing at the same time.

I want to open my eyes but can't. Something feels wrong. I imagine myself standing, both feet firmly planted on the ground, yet my stomach is frozen at the wrong angle, stuck mid-flip.

Then something shifts and my stomach lands, just not in an orientation where I think 'up' is. My body adapts automatically, reorienting into alignment, and all my joints click into place, equilibrium flooding my senses with queasy certainty.

I relax slightly and take a deep, shuddering breath of fresh air. It doesn't help. A cold sweat erupts from my skin. Placing one hand over my abused stomach and the other over my riotous heart, I try to keep both organs from bursting out of my chest like an alien from that old Sigourney Weaver film. "Seriously, Anubis," I groan. "You can't kill a girl and resurrect her only to scare her to death immediately afterward. I'm pretty sure that's classified as a dick move."

He doesn't reply – no surprise – and it takes me forever to feel confident enough to move without vomiting. Eventually, my equilibrium stops weaving like a drunk staggering from a bar at two a.m., and I finally open my eyes.

The juxtaposition between the rough earthen caves of Duat to a bright and extremely opulent bathroom is so intense that I blink several times to make sure I'm not hallucinating. The walls and floor are slabs of light-brown marble, lined with veins of dark brown, white, black, and gold, but the ceiling is a rich green, mottled with similar browns and blacks. The countertops lining two of the walls match, and the mirrors above make the already impressively sized room seem even larger. Opaque glass circles in the ceiling release a torrent of white natural light that floods the room.

Spinning around, I take in the individual details together and realize the design creates an illusion of an ancient forest caught in daylight. Even the stalls add to the effect, doors and walls running floor to ceiling in the

3

same marble, secured by bronze locks that blend in with the brown, creating a thicket of trees where one could privately do their business.

The only thing that feels out of place is the door – tucked away in a corner between the two countertops – and a vintage red chaise lounge flanked by two matching armchairs sitting on one side of the room, set up in a conversational way around a low, wooden coffee table. "So fancy," I exhale, completely awestruck by the exquisite taste of the designer.

My tongue sticks to the roof of my mouth and I realize how parched I am. *How long have I been dead,* I wonder. *Can a spirit get dehydrated?*

I'm not sure and I really don't care. My gaze focuses on the sinks set into the countertop. Moving over to one, I lift the lever of the well-style faucet, releasing a stream of clear water, and place my mouth directly on the man-made waterfall, greedily slurping it down. It's delicious and refreshing, and I drink like it's been days since I've had a taste.

Eventually, the cold of the marble bleeds into my chest, and I pull away with a hiss as my nipples contract to painful points. Straightening, I glance at myself in the mirror, then double-take at the disastrous reflection peering back at me. Dark hair sticks out in wild, uneven tangles pointing every direction but down, and my skin is streaked with black earth slashing through the golden remnants of the Egyptian hieroglyphics Anubis painted on me. I look like I've climbed out of a grave.

Adding insult to injury, I'm completely nude under those earthen skid marks, devoid of even a scrap of fabric to cover my bushy mound. My mouth draws in a thin, displeased line and I flex my hands, trying very hard not to lose my shit. Admittedly, I asked Anubis to send me to my next paramour but being sent without clothes is a big oversight. One that feels intentional given what I'd seen of the god's power.

"Anubis!" I shout, letting my voice reverberate off the walls. "Clothes! Now! Or the next time I see you, I'll come after you with a rolled-up newspaper!" It's a silly threat to throw at a jackal-headed god, but I hope it's insulting enough to get a response.

Don't lie – you just want to fuck him again, VJ – the personification I've given my lady-bits – croons, clenching vaginal muscles together in a ravenous flex. *You want to feel him stretching us out with that massive head of his, splitting us in half, making us come over and over again until we're sopping wet and boneless.*

I grab onto the edge of the countertop to keep upright, the flash of heat pouring through my body hot enough to make my skeletal structure melt. *How can you still be this turned on,* I think at her incredulously. Her answer is a silent, hungry pulse, causing me to clench my knees together lest they fall open and I masturbate right there on the bathroom floor. *I just had sex! Mind-blowing, life-affirming sex! I just...*

Images from the past twenty-four hours flood my mind, from meeting Hermes and learning the ancient gods of mythology are real to being strangled by Anubis while he ate me out. "I can't believe I did that,"

5

I exhale, shaking my head back and forth in disbelief. "I can't believe I..."

It's too much to put into words, and a part of me is afraid speaking them aloud will only affirm how crazy it all is. *I died. Went to the underworld and confronted my demons. Stood up to Jason, the worst ex in the world, and finally told him off. Had anal sex with the Egyptian god of death in a crazy resurrection ritual.*

"Did I do this?" I ask, meeting my own gaze in the mirror. A smile tugs at my lips. "Is this really me?"

The confidence is so foreign that doubts immediately rise to slap it down. *You're just riding an endorphin high,* they whisper. *You almost died in Duat when you threw yourself off the boat. Anubis wouldn't even touch you before he sent you away – probably because you're bad in bed. He's probably already telling whoever's next to –*

Shut the fuck up, VJ screams, cutting through the noise with a sharp squeeze of my channel. *We're here for one reason and one reason only: To get good and thoroughly fucked.* My lust returns in a flash – too many years of self-inflicted orgasms only fueling the insatiable beast between my thighs – and I can't stop the torrent of memories tearing through me.

I struggle to catch my breath, the pleasure too intense to allow my basic motor functions to operate. Bit by bit, my ass relaxes, opening under the unrelenting force of his tapered head and the conflicting pleasure building within VJ. Each millimeter deeper into my rectum is one she can feel through the thin wall separating the two, and she – we – are so… fucking… close.

"More," I beg, bearing down on his dick and relaxing my asshole as much as I can.

Anubis groans low in his throat, his finger stopping and pressing down on my clit. The pressure rockets through VJ, causing her to sputter and shake on the cusp of orgasm, and his cock slips into me with an inaudible pop.

He freezes, but I squirm, caught between the pleasure and pain of something so wide being lodged so deeply into my ass. I'm stuffed, yet so empty. VJ can feel the heavy press of his cock, and pulses in abject loneliness, longing to be filled as completely as my ass.

"M-m-more," I cry, a whimper and demand tied together in the same syllable.

He replies by pushing my hips down, driving the burning knot deeper. A choked cry escapes my lips, I forget how to breathe, lost in the sensation of the bulb-shaped head tunneling deep into me. The sensation is different – not pleasure exactly – but not painful either. More concentrated than both but adding up to a desperate throbbing with no sign of abating. I wiggle and squirm, the fight for friction and an end to the mounting tension twisting me up tighter than a parachute cord, ready to be pulled

I break down and beg, unable to stand the madness. "Please! Finish it!"

"Almost," Anubis growls.

The creak of a door opening rips me from my

fantasy, and I jerk toward the only entrance to the room. It's still closed, but the sharp click-clack of approaching heels behind it tells me it won't be for long. *Oh shit. Is the next one I'm meeting a goddess?* My leg muscles tighten; I know I only have seconds to hide.

I dart into a stall and close the door quickly, locking it tight, then brace my shoulder against it for good measure. *Thankfully there's no gap between the floor and the walls. Otherwise, I'd have to climb on top of the toilet, and I'm too old for that middle school shit.*

The door opens a heartbeat later. I hold my breath as a rhythmic *tck, tck, tck* noise fills the room, drawing closer and closer. For a heartbeat, I'm certain the person on the other side has come for me. Then a stall door creaks open, closes with a thump, and there's a sharp *click* of a lock sliding into place. Clothing rustles, then the steady sound of peeing fills the room.

Of course they're here to use the bathroom, I think, cheeks burning. *It's clearly a public restroom!* I exhale in relief and try to get my heart to slow, convincing myself everything's fine.

My bladder chooses that exact moment to alert me it's dangerously full, the sound of urination and my earlier drinking causing pain so intense, I press my thighs together to keep from pissing on the floor.

Fuck, right now? I clench everything tight, trying to fight the urge, but can feel a drop trying to break through, bladder too full to be denied. *Can't it wait? This chick is going to freak out if she thinks she's alone then hears me taking a wee!*

My body doesn't care, and I feel control quickly slipping. I barely get a chance to sit before the stream is clattering against the porcelain bowl below. Wincing, I quickly pinch off the stream and hold my breath, ears straining for the slightest rustle from my stall mate. Her stream continues, unabated, and I let go of the breath I'm holding.

Pressing my thick thighs together to cover the bowl, I tilt my hips back as far as possible and resume peeing. My eyelashes flutter closed, both in relief of release as well as the noticeably muffled sound. For several long seconds, I savor the sensation, before my introspective nature begins examining my ridiculous antics.

Seriously, why am I even acting like this? It's not like she can see me, and as far as hearing me goes... It's the restroom! The place where you're absolutely allowed to pee!

Well, it doesn't help that Anubis dropped us here buck ass naked, another voice retorts. I nod while reaching for a handful of toilet paper.

That's a good point, but I mean... What am I even doing here? I shake my head. *I thought facing Jason was going to make me more confident, but here I am, hiding in a bathroom stall and masking the sound of my pee because I'm too insecure about my nudity and recently-been-shagged hair!*

Well, what are we supposed to do, a different part inquires. *Stick around and try to explain?! Walk into whatever public area exists on the other side of that door*

9

Mona Ventress

like nothing's wrong?

The thought is coated with sarcasm, but despite it, my mind immediately conjures up an image of myself strutting into a room completely naked, filled with another man's spunk and confident enough to own it. For one spectacular second, I imagine being in *that* Delilah's shoes, a version of myself that's strong, proud, and indifferent to what others think.

Then reality returns, bringing with it the certainty that I'll never be her. My shoulders slump, exhaustion and depression heavy weights stamping me down. Anubis gave me the option to go home and rest, and while I had initially refused – riding high on the first good sex I'd had in years and VJ's never-ending quest to be filled beyond capacity – I'm thinking I made a mistake.

The toilet across from me lets out a gurgling roar, jerking me back to reality. I clench off the remaining drops of pee as the stall door creaks open. Heels clack against the marble but come to a sudden stop after a handful of steps. Holding my breath, I remain still as the sound of running water from a faucet fills the room. My bladder pulses angrily, but I ignore it and wait while the stranger washes their hands and leaves. I hear a blast of deep, thrumming electronica music as they exit, then the door closes, and all is silent again.

I relax and release the rest of my urine, using the time to dissect my problems. Anubis hasn't answered me yet, so either he can't hear me, or he can't come. There's only one door in and out, and I'm not confident enough to walk out those doors in my current state. I

10

could already picture the mixture of concern and speculation being directed toward me and know I wouldn't be able to handle the scrutiny without dissolving into tears.

I could use the sinks to wash up, but clothes are going to be an issue. Maybe I can do something with the cushions? I assume they're washable, which means I can probably remove the covering and… I dismiss the idea seconds later, realizing I have no way of cutting additional holes in the fabric for my head or limbs.

I eye the toilet paper. It's an expensive brand, but on a standard-sized roll, with only one replacement hanging above it. With six stalls, there are twelve rolls of toilet paper. It's possibly enough to cover my generous curves, but without a way to secure it, there is no guarantee it wouldn't fall to pieces after a few steps.

VJ whines, clenching muscles in our abdomen to remind us of the hollow ache inside. Urinating has helped relieve some of the intensity, but her demand is clear: She hungers.

"Not sure what to tell you," I inform the source of my displeasure in a low voice. "With my two options being sofa cushion extravaganza or toilet paper chic, the only way I'm leaving this stall is through divine intervention."

"Did someone mention divine intervention?" a deep and completely un-expected voice asks.

Chapter Two

I scream as a tall man with olive skin and gold springy hair materializes inside the stall. Reacting as any red-blooded female would, I clench my knees together, bend forward to obscure my nudity, and throw a hard right hook.

To my surprise, it lands squarely in his crotch with a thud resonating all the way up my shoulder. My eyes widen and I withdraw my fist. Glancing up, I'm surprised to see his face turn a shocking hue of red, then purple, before finally bleeding away to an ashen gray. A low, pained gurgle escapes his throat, and he reaches down with both hands to cradle his groin while simultaneously waddling backward. The door behind him evaporates before he touches it, but he only makes it a few more steps before he collapses on the floor.

"I think you killed me," he chokes out, rocking

side to side.

Tears leak from blue-green eyes brighter than the Mediterranean Sea, and even though he is clearly in pain, I can't fight the laughter bubbling up from my stomach. "It serves you right, Hermes," I chide. Spreading my thighs just enough to wipe, I find just enough sass to add, "Next time, appear on the other side of the door and knock like a fucking gentleman."

"Duly noted," the Greek messenger god wheezes. I wait for him to say more, but all he does is continue to cradle his family jewels, groaning as if I've gelded him. I roll my eyes at his theatrics, but inside, a seed of doubt blossoms. *Did I really hurt him that much? Could I? He is a god, isn't he?*

I swear, if you've ruined his dick for us, I will make our panties look like the bloody elevator from The Shining for years to come, VJ growls.

You don't have that kind of power, I shoot back, but can't help the sliver of guilt breaking through my righteous humor. Standing up, I flush, I quickly rinse my hands at the sink then make my way to him. "Are you okay?" I ask, kneeling.

His head bobs in short little jerks, making the tight ringlets of hair bounce. My fingers itch to reach out and slide my fingers through the corkscrews, but I keep them pressed against my knee. "Totally fine," he wheezes in a way that makes me laugh. He smiles despite the pain and gingerly releases his crotch to sit up.

Leaning back on my heels, I watch him,

suddenly struck by how similar the situation is to when I first met him. *Granted, I'd been clothed then, but no less vulnerable, and reacted similarly by swinging a bat at his head, and he'd...*

My thought train stalls at the recollection, the jarring difference between then and now confusing me. "How the hell was I able to hit you? The last time I tried, you turned my bat into flowers."

"Oh." Hermes blinks at me in surprise, then offers a lopsided grin. "Last time, you asked me not to read your thoughts anymore, so this time I didn't." His eyes catch mine and the flames within them consume all the oxygen in my lungs.

Oh god, is he respecting my boundaries? That's so fucking hot. Why is that so fucking hot? VJ clenches in agreement, keeping the rush of wetness his simple admission causes from dripping down my thighs. "I... Thank you?" I stammer, breaking eye contact. The intensity of how quickly my attraction ratchets up for him is frightening, and I automatically try to distract from it by changing the topic. "What are you doing here? Is it... Is it our turn?" Every cell in my body goes silent as I wait for his answer.

"Not yet, precious," Hermes whispers. A pang of sadness ripples through me as he continues. "Anubis let me know he sent you ahead early, so I came to give Bacchus a head's up." He runs a hand through his hair and gifts me with a rakish smile that threatens to make VJ pop like a balloon. "I heard you talking to yourself and figured I'd see how you were feeling about everything, but now I'm worried the answer isn't positive? What's going on, darling? How can I help?"

I bite my lower lip, frightened by how much I want to open up to him. I've been hurt before by being honest about what I want, so keeping people at arm's length is second nature to me. Yet with him, I can't seem to stop myself. "I don't know, just... After Anubis, I felt strong, confident, and... starved." My cheeks heat and I risk a glance at him, expecting judgment. He simply meets my gaze, patiently waiting. My heart flip-flops in my chest, making it difficult to breathe. "I told him I wanted more, but then he sent me here completely naked and I..." I pause to clear my throat. "I'm tired and filthy and just feel like..." I trail off again, unable to articulate exactly how I'm feeling.

"You feel like what?"

I flounder. I hate being vulnerable like this. Years of living with my mom has made emotional expression terrifying, and life with Jason has only reinforced that behavior.

But we're supposed to be past that, a voice inside reminds. *And he's asking. Just... try.*

Exhaling slowly, I close my eyes and relent, mouth falling open and letting the truth tumble out. "I feel like what I did to face Jason doesn't matter and I'll just be the same insecure and broken Delilah forever." I wait for Hermes to say something – to agree or disagree – but once again, he is silent, like he knows there is more. He's not wrong, so I swallow hard and ask, "Can you... can you send me home?" in a small voice, hating myself for taking the coward's way out.

He doesn't physically react, but I can sense a change in him, a sudden urgent undertone that wasn't there before. "You want to leave?" he asks. His voice betrays nothing, but even still, my instincts scream for me to choose my words very carefully, like he fears my response.

"Well, not forever," I hastily explain. "It's just…" I look down at the dirt coating my skin, then thrust out my hands to him, "Look at me! I'm filthy, my hair is disgusting, and I'm leaking – " I slam my mouth shut, incapable of admitting anything about the status of my bunghole, and change tactics. "I need a shower, Hermes. I need clothes. I may seem confident being all naked in front of you, but I'm not! Inside, I'm a fucking mess."

Tears form, making the bottom of my vision waver. I reach up with both hands to hide my face from him, but his hands grab my wrists and hold me back. I look up at him in surprise, and he leverages it against me to pull me against the wall of his chest and hug me tight.

"Your shirt," I sniffle, remembering the pristine white fabric and pushing away. VJ resists, crying out, *We're laying on top of him, idiot! This is the perfect position to ride him to oblivion and back.* Her observation is dwarfed by the fear, joy, relief, and pleasure as the arms around me tighten, flipping between them like a dryer set to tumble.

"Fuck it," he replies, his voice a rumble in my ear. "I'd rather be covered in dirt and holding you than clean any day of the week."

17

My face flushes, vision blurring with unshed tears. His words make me feel so special, even though I know I'm not. "Why?" I find myself asking. One leaks out and drips on his shirt, and I roll my eyes and try to blink the rest back. "Why do you care?"

"I have my reasons." I open my mouth to demand more, but he silences me with a soft, "Shhhhhh. I promise I'll tell you about them one day, but right now, I'm just here to make sure you feel safe and comfortable. Speaking of which..." He lifts one hand in the air and twists it around with a little flourish.

Something slides between us so fast that I sit up with a gasp. It follows me as I move, and I look down at my chest as black fabric slides over my breasts and shoulders, lifting the twins and fixing them in place. I stand and spin toward the mirror, watching as an elegant black A-line dress with a halter top manifests around me. The dirt streaking my body lifts off and evaporates mid-air, while my hair smooths and straightens, growing lustrous and full.

For several seconds, all I do is stare at the familiar-looking stranger my reflection makes. There are fewer flaws in my complexion, the normal collection of red bumps smoothed away into an even tone. My face is framed by thick glossy dark curls. Everywhere I look, I find some small change – the cleft in my chin slightly deeper and the shape of my lips fuller – but it's my eyes I keep coming back to, the normal muddy brown replaced by intense obsidian irises that glitter magnetically.

"What's going on?" I breathe, touching my cheek,

unable to believe the reflection staring back at me. "Did you do something to me?"

"Not at all," he chuckles, tiny wings on his shoes coming to life with a sharp buzz and lifting him off the floor. "You healed some of the pain scarring your heart." He reaches out with both hands and brushes my hair off my shoulders.

My spine shudders at the contact, and VJ clenches in a slow pull, throwing up fantasies of Hermes and me locked together in an embrace, his cock swelling inside of me, filling us completely. He moves in slow, unhurried strokes, depth and speed increasing in response to my non-verbal cues, building to a detonation so intense, I go blind.

"You'd be surprised how much of an effect such a catharsis can have on your physical presence."

His voice is a hot whisper in my ear, and I almost choke on saliva at the intensity of my need for him. My eyes snap open to find his lips inches from my neck and I fight a visceral reaction to tilt my head and offer myself to him as a human sacrifice. My nostrils fill with his scent – salt, the ocean, and a soft floral smell I still can't identify – and I grab the sink for support.

The rules, I remind myself sternly, recalling the dire warning he'd given me on our first meeting about how there is an order to these encounters. Meeting his gaze in the mirror, I turn, his name a whisper on my lips. I want to tell him to stop, but it all falls away as he steps into me, boxing me in against the counter.

"Change is never a straightforward path, Delilah."

My eyes flutter closed, heart tap dancing out of alignment with the normal rhythm. "You've unburdened yourself of a deep and significant pain, yes, but it does not mean you are whole. Something must fill the void where the pain was, and you must decide what it's going to be. That takes time."

I want it to be you, VJ cries, and all the cells in my body scream in agreement. The only thing that doesn't is a colder, more jaded part of myself, one already dissecting his words like a coroner investigating whether the corpse was murdered.

Is he right, I wonder. *Or is he just saying that because he wants me to continue? Does he only want me to persevere until it's his turn, and will he abandon me after he gets what he wants, just like everyone else has?*

VJ rejects the idea outright, but my instincts can't, the past too visceral to ever truly forget. *He's omitted the truth once already. How could I take anything at face value again?* Shaking my head to clear it from the warm fuzzy sensation his proximity creates, I slide out from under his arm and move away, carving a little distance between us before I ask.

"Hermes…" I begin, picking at my cuticles. "Why didn't you tell me that Anubis had to kill me before this whole arrangement could kick off?"

Chapter Three

Aquamarine eyes widen in surprise, and he takes a step back. "I..." He looks away, rubbing the back of his head with one hand, and I realize my question has caught him completely off-guard, confirming he hasn't been reading my mind.

Suddenly, I'm torn in half, conflicted by his reaction. I want to preen with joy that he continues to respect my boundaries, but I can't let myself, not while his body language screams 'guilty.' The urge to demand more information is strong, yet I remember the patience he greeted me with earlier and try to reciprocate. The air between us turns thick with tension as the seconds tick by, and I hold my breath, worried I'll miss his response.

Eventually, he meets my gaze, the twin blue-green pools pleading for clemency. "You must understand. You're the first human we've invited to do this in almost two centuries. A rare mix of several elements and traits not easily made manifest in the mortal world. After I met you... I couldn't risk you saying 'no.' I didn't want to."

Uncertainty bubbles in my chest. I take a healthy step back, re-evaluating the man in front of me.

His face goes ashen, and he raises a hand. "I'm sorry. I know... I should've told you – I should've! But I also knew if I mentioned needing to die so that we could prepare your body for sex with us, you'd decline immediately."

"Yeah," I reply, voice sour with sarcasm. "It turns out I like being fully informed of things before I agree to them. I'm kind of weird like that."

Hermes flinches. "You're right," he mutters, hunching his shoulders. "I shouldn't have done it. I just...." He lifts his head, meeting my gaze, and the want spilling from those beautiful twin seas makes an involuntary rush of answering lust surge through my channel, taking both me and VJ by surprise. My breath evaporates in my lungs, and I must breathe twice as hard to keep from growing faint.

How can a single look make me feel like this, I question, searching for a shred of rationale. *How can I feel so attracted when I barely know him? When he's already lied?!*

My nostrils flare and hands ball into fists, rage burning a clean line through a libido willing to get in the way of demanding the respect and honesty I deserve.

"You've already lied once, Hermes. Why should I believe you're being honest now? How can I?"

He opens his mouth, shuts it with a click, then bobs his head in small, jerky nods. "You're right. I'll... I'll let the others know what I did. They'll probably dissolve the agreement and send you home, but that's only fair since I misled you."

My eyes widen in alarm as he starts to turn away, and I grab his wrist to stop him from leaving. "No!" I blurt out, voice hoarse. Stopping, he looks down at my hand, and I let go of him quickly, not wanting him to mistake my denial for something more.

For several seconds, neither of us says anything, and I recognize he's waiting for me to explain, but am not sure why I said 'no' in the first place. The move had been instinctual; a response to the idea of stopping after everything I'd accomplished in Duat. Something has awakened inside – a deep hunger and curiosity to see where this road will take me, and I just couldn't bear it if it ended over this. "I... I want to keep going," I finally say, filling the space between us.

Golden eyebrows lift in surprise, then lower. "Oh, of course," he replies, ducking his head. "Then I'll have myself removed from the situation. It's only right, all things considered."

The breath I couldn't catch earlier completely evaporates in my lungs, and the world goes gray at the edges. *No Hermes?* Both VJ and I can't imagine the possibility. My heart pounds against my breastbone, panic mounting at the idea of the first man who exhibited even the slightest regard for my boundaries suddenly being absent from this whole experience. I think quickly, looking for a way to backpedal out of this, a way I can live with, even in the face of his lie.

Clearing my throat, I say "I don't think that's necessary," trying to keep my tone as non-committal as possible. "If you promise never to do it again, and – "

"I promise." He interjects immediately, turning toward me, a small line burrowing between his eyebrows. "I won't ever – "

"You need to shut up and let me finish before you go making promises," I interject, the anger in my tone barely leashed. "It makes me feel like you're not really listening."

"Right. Sorry." He takes steps back and waits, giving me space to speak.

That small act – more than anything else – bolsters my confidence that I'm doing the right thing. "As I was saying, not only will you agree to never lie to me again, but you also have to answer any questions I have about this whole arrangement, no matter what."

He hesitates, then looks around the room, as if checking we're alone. "I'll do my best, but I'm not exactly supposed to be here right now. If I linger too long, they'll – "

I sigh noisily, interrupting him. It's a refrain I've already heard before, which means he's wasting time. "They'll make you forfeit your turn with me, *blah blah blah*." I give him a pointed look while tapping my wrist with an index finger. "Then let's not waste this moment. Why are the gods so interested in humans? Have all the goddesses finally figured out what a bunch of turds they are and are just over it?"

Hermes emits a sharp bark of laughter, but it disappears quickly behind a wave of pain. "I'm sorry," he says, shaking his head. "It would be nice if that were the reason, but the reality is far grimmer. You see, there aren't many of our female counterparts left alive. Many died off as their followers were persecuted and destroyed, and those who did survive only did so through their marriages to other, more powerful deities, or from those scant humans who survived and were brave enough to maintain their faith in secrecy."

"Holy shit," I say. Somehow, his answer makes sense, but I also can't help the pang of loss accompanying it, unable to feel anything but robbed of the chance to meet a strong and powerful goddess. "That's terrible." I bite my lip, thinking, then recall something from the haphazard research I'd done after meeting him. "What about the nymphs? Didn't Zeus and the other gods get it on with them all the time?"

"Absolutely, all the time. Their bodies were better equipped to handle us, and…" He trails off, gaze growing distant and lips lifting in a smile, as if trapped in a pleasant memory. "… they were always into what we wanted to try, no matter what. Even humans had some hard limits, but not our nymphs. Which made it even more devastating when they were wiped out."

"How did it happen?" I ask, curiosity getting the better of me.

25

He shrugs. "Everyone's got theories, but no one really knows for certain. Some think they angered Zeus by denying him. Others think it was retaliation from some of the hybrid species, angered over mankind's dominance of the planet. Even more believe it was the humans themselves, although they squabble over which faction was ultimately responsible. In any case, those that remain are… taken, so to speak, which makes our options for romantic liaisons extremely limited."

"I see." It isn't exactly flattering, learning I'm a choice made from lack of options. If anything, it seems sad and pathetic, and suddenly I'm reconsidering my participation.

Something in my face or voice must've revealed my disappointment to Hermes, because he blurts, "It's not like that. The gods have been having liaisons with humans long before these events, but as the world changed and knowledge of our kind was eradicated, we had to adapt accordingly. This is just… one of the ways we did so." He pauses, waiting for me to react, but when I don't, adds, "Believe me, our choice in you goes far deeper than necessity, Delilah."

"Right," I scoff. "Like not being a virgin, but also being done with lovers altogether?"

He doesn't flinch this time. "Yes. Among a lot of other things."

"What things? And why?"

"I…" he trails off, jaw flexing with uncertainty. "I honestly don't know. I'm just the messenger, Delilah. I was only ever supposed to have that one interaction with you until it was our time together. I know the traits I requested, but that's about it."

"What did you request? Why even do this? Isn't being with one person once over however many years just… depressing?" The questions fall out of me before I can think them through. Maybe I don't want to hear this, I think, but it's too late – Hermes keeps his promise to be honest.

"Someone smart. Funny. Com-passionate." His eyes meet mine, once again carrying a heat that instantly evaporates all my doubts, filling me with a warmth that makes my skin glow. "And because, at the end of the day, we're lonely, and could use some companionship, even if it's just for a little while."

"Oh." It's all I can muster in response, my entire focus on supplying my runaway heart with enough oxygen so it doesn't explode in my chest. I ache for the longing in his voice and fight VJ's demand we physically comfort him right there on the spot. That means there's no chance for a relationship either, I inform her, which only intensifies the pain in my chest.

The rules, I remind myself sharply, trying to distract from the inexplicable hurt his revelation brings. *Just focus on learning the rules of the arrangement, not about finding 'the one.' I mean c'mon – the gods only invited you to fuck, not to date. Get it together, Hansen.* I'm right, but the pain is still there, begging me to ask if there's a chance for us. *We barely even know him,* I think, pushing it away. *And he lied.*

It doesn't make the desire fade.

27

"Hermes," I start, mind scrabbling for literally any other subject. It finally lands on something, and I don't hesitate to articulate it. "Earlier, when I asked you to take me home, it felt like you were afraid of my answer. Why?"

He hesitates and looks away, shoulders rising and falling like the tides. "Oh. You, uh… caught that, huh?"

"Well, you did request someone smart, so…" I trail off, rocking back and forth on my feet, and somehow, a small smile works its way through my wariness and mistrust.

His features soften, and he smiles back a little. "I guess I did, huh?" Raking a hand through his hair, he turns away and begins pacing. "Look, this doesn't exactly paint my kind in a great light, but one of the stipulations of the agreement states that once you arrive in our domain, you must stay until you learn what our desires are. After that, you're free to opt-out, but to do so beforehand is tantamount to a rejection of the entire arrangement."

My brows draw together. "What? That's the stupidest thing I've ever heard! You're telling me the gods can't handle being asked to reschedule? Seriously?"

"That's not fair," Hermes retorts, spinning around. "We're shaped by those who believe in us, Delilah, which means we are as flawed as any other human, just to a more intense degree. Many of us are sheer egomaniacs due to those who followed us, then became dark and twisted when our myths were tainted through propaganda and fearmongering." I raise an eyebrow at the admission, and Hermes rolls his eyes and throws his arms in the air. "Not me, of course, but you know the stories! We can be petty and thoughtless and, yeah, we take things personally. Rejection, especially after how far some of us have fallen, is devastating."

"Okay," I begin, then pause. I'm not sure what this information reveals, other than a group of ancient gods were self-aware enough to create rules for their sex-capades, yet not enough to let their participants leave if they needed to rest. I consider this for a few seconds. "To be clear, I can still say no at any time after I learn what they want or get uncomfortable, yes? And I'll still have an opportunity to meet with someone else?"

"Yes," he says in a solemn voice. "Your consent is important to us." He opens his mouth as if he wants to say something else but suddenly looks over his shoulder instead, as if he hears something I can't. "I know you have more questions, Delilah, but we need to wrap it up. If I don't leave soon, Bacchus will get suspicious and come to investigate."

The name rings a bell, but I can't quite place it. "That's the second time you've said that name – who is he?"

Hermes rolls his eyes. "A drama king in my opinion, but one of his domains is theater, and another is drinking, so... I'm not entirely wrong. You probably know him as Dionysus. That's what the Greeks called him, anyway."

His Greek name immediately triggers a connection to Bacchus that takes me back to my college days, in the form of the only frat party I ever attended: A Bacchanalia – a giant, orgiastic party in worship of the Roman god of wine, Bacchus. I'd been so overwhelmed by the sight of people having sex in the open that I'd immediately left, then masturbated about it endlessly for weeks to come, wishing I'd had the guts to participate.

And here I am, over a decade later, presented with a chance to make my fantasy a reality. My doubts multiply into a thousand bats fluttering wildly in my stomach. "He's going to make me have sex in public, isn't he?"

Hermes hooks a finger under my chin, lifting my head until I meet his gaze. "Yes, but you and I know it's something you've fantasized about endlessly." I flush, embarrassed by how much he knows, and he murmurs, "I promise, that's one I got from before you asked me to stop."

I bite my lip and glance up at him from beneath my eyelashes to find him smiling warmly at me. "I honestly can't wait to see how you do. If I'm lucky, he may ask me to join, and then we can have a little fun in advance, yeah?"

VJ melts down faster than a nuclear power plant, molten liquid heat spilling past my lips and saturating the curls covering them. "He can do that?" I whisper.

His grin deepens, revealing a perfect set of

glistening white teeth. "He absolutely can, but even if he doesn't... don't you deserve to know what it feels like to be on display, the center of attention?"

Shifting my weight back and forth, I search for the strength to agree, but my nerves are already getting the better of me. "I... I feel like I'm supposed to say 'yes' here, but I really don't know, Hermes. Fantasies are one thing, but reality... Reality is another."

He cocks his head, then nods. "Just try, precious. That's all we ask."

I open my mouth to protest, but he silences me by pressing his lips to mine. I exhale in surprise as his silky-smooth curves fit against mine in the gentlest of presses. Then he is gone, ankle-wings carrying him toward the ceiling so fast it creates a torrent of wind that makes my skirt whip so dangerously high on my thighs, I have to use both hands to keep them down. For a moment, I'm Marilyn Monroe over that vent, but it disappears as Hermes does, his image evaporating from sight an instant before he hits the wall.

Staring after him for several seconds, my fingers skim where we had touched in the sweetest of kisses, savoring the soft glow it leaves inside. It doesn't last long, a voice reminding me that I'm here for someone else, but for the moment it's there, it's nicer than anything I've felt in a long time.

Turning back to the mirror, I shake the encounter from my mind and focus on the task at hand. "Hermes is right. I've had fantasies about being fucked in front of other people, and this is my chance to see if it lives up

31

to my imagination."

My stomach churns and lungs catch, mind already convinced it won't, VJ screaming it will, and me trapped between them both. I swallow hard to forcibly remove the lump of doubt lodged in my throat, but it only moves a few scant millimeters, clinging in place like toxic sludge.

I try again, refusing to back down. "We're different now. We get to be different. No one out there knows who we are, so why not be the confident woman we've always wished we were? And, if anything gets too crazy, we can tell him no, and leave, no biggie."

Somehow, this collection of words helps, and I use the surge of confidence to head to the door.

Yay, VJ cries, walls flexing as if she were trying to clap. *We'll get to fuck Bacchus and Hermes at the same time! We can finally try that double penetration thing we've always fantasized about.*

Muscles clench, reacting to the fantasy of being stuffed in both holes. *Hermes in front of me, mystery man Bacchus behind, and suddenly, my fears seem so small when compared to the massive beast that is my lust. Being pressed between two men as they move in and out of me, gliding in slick unison until I break on them over and over and over again...*

I brace the wall for balance, knees suddenly weak from want. "Keep it together," I growl, willing my legs to remain firm beneath me. Taking a moment to collect myself, I wobble out the door, propelled forward like a lust-fueled rocket on a mission to explode.

The bathroom door leads to a narrow hall on a downward incline and doubles back on itself before ending in a second, matching door. A pulsing rhythm vibrates through the thick wood, so strong it bounces inside the frame. I can't hear anything else but knowing there's a Bacchanalia on the other side has my skin crawling under the weight of all the bodies waiting, ready to fall like an avalanche on my head. My burst of bravado vanishes, and anxiety blooms in their absence. I'm frozen, unable to take another step forward or even risk opening the door.

I take a deep breath and push it down. *I thought we were done with this, but for the last time: This is your chance to be different, Delilah. You're ready for this, you deserve this, and you can go home at any time.*

My hand quivers as I reach up and I have to grab the door handle just to make it stop. The metal feels wrong in my hands. Alien. I know it's just my panic, telling me to run and hide, and for once in my life, I don't want to listen. That story always has the same ending; me alone, without anyone to touch or be beside. I starve for affection. Crave attention.

I stare at the wood for a long moment. Then I turn the handle, pull it open, and throw all caution to the wind.

Chapter Four

Sound pours through the void like a physical force, so strong I can feel it pulsating from the soles of my feet to the roots of my hair. Bright, colorful lights flash in time with the beat, making it hard to see through the kaleidoscope of green, blue, purple, red, orange, and yellow. Lifting a hand to shade my eyes, I step over the threshold to get a better view.

People undulate in front of me, fervently dancing to the heavy electronica beat. Clouds of artificial smoke waft through the room, obscuring entire areas and reducing every being inside to wraith-like shadows that loom large. Like a moth to the flame, I enter the sea of flesh, too absorbed by the glowing patterns and music to fully register the individuals around me.

The lights change, the multi-spectral colors

shifting to a bluish-white strobe that flashes in time with a rapidly building backbeat, so fast that the dancers' sinuous movements become disconnected images. The anticipation mounts, the promise of a bass drop tantalizingly close, when the music cuts off and the room goes pitch black.

The deafening silence stretches on long enough to make me wonder, *Did the power go out or did the lights and volume make me deaf and blind?* when bright lights snap on and the music returns, bass hitting so hard that VJ clenches in pleasure.

The crowd screams their approval to the DJ – now illuminated in an elevated booth only a few feet away – and double-time their dance moves to the beat. I lose all sight of them, too astonished by the alien blending of human and animal characteristics of the DJ to focus on anything else.

The shape is distinctly humanoid; there are two arms, a torso, and a head. They're also wearing clothes – a T-shirt covers a flat chest, and there's a cap secured by a large pair of headphones. But it's the long green snout nearly two feet in length and lined with wickedly curved inch-long teeth that holds my eyes captive. One scaled arm ending in six fingers tipped with talons moves in time with the beat under a banner reading 'DJ Death Roll' in graphic neon green and pink spray paint. A thick, reptilian tail rises behind it, the tip bobbing from shoulder to shoulder.

I'm frozen, but my mind blurs into activity with a flurry of questions. *There are alligator gods? Or is it a crocodile? If it's a crocodile, it'd be Egyptian, wouldn't it?*

Why would an Egyptian god be a DJ? Does Anubis know they're alive? Oh no, is that what Bacchus looks like?

Something slams into me, derailing my crashing thought train. I stumble toward a pair of dancers but catch my balance before I crash into them. Taking a deep breath, I whirl around to give the bumper a stern, 'watch it,' but stop when I see a bipedal stag staring at me with wide, apologetic eyes.

He lifts a pair of cloven hooves to either side of his mouth, and bellows an inaudible, "Sorry," through furry lips and small flat teeth. My gaze slides down his body, taking in the black leather straps crisscrossing a human torso and ending in bikini underwear seated between two delicate hindquarters. He turns toward me and something long and thin swings into view from between his bowed legs. I look away as heat builds in my cheeks.

Before VJ can insist we turn and openly ogle the creature, a blue female wearing a red, skin-tight, vinyl dress catches my eye. She commands the small space she dances in, arms and hips undulating with fluidic motions, while her legs stamp out a fierce walk that keeps the growing crowd back. She's bald, save for a fin-like crest rising from the top of her skull, and gorgeous, evidenced by the loose semi-circle of men and women around her. Each vies for her attention, from a male fairy with bright orange and black butterfly wings to a large bear standing on its hind legs. As my gaze falls on the hulking mass, it reaches up to its face and...

My jaw drops as the head pulls back and the

37

bear deflates, turning into a pale woman with white hair and striking blue eyes, a bear's pelt draped over delicate shoulders. *What are all these creatures*, I wonder, unable to keep from blatantly staring.

The azure woman ignores them all, her focus completely riveted on a tall shark-man wearing leather straps like the stag-man wears. He is massive – easily twice her size – and completely top-heavy, his chest and arms ripped and covered with spiraling tribal tattoos that look Polynesian in design. *A shark deity, maybe? God, I wish I'd studied more mythology in school.*

The thought is immediately forgotten as the woman circles him, her hands gliding over his rubbery gray and white flesh. She disappears behind him, but I can still see her long, shapely legs between his splayed, scrawny ones, knees bending forward as she kneels.

VJ throbs as the fish-lady thrusts a hand between his thighs, palming his groin through the fabric. Her hand barely fits over the thick bulge, making my mouth go dry. Slowly, she rubs up and down while burying her face in his ass, and his phallus swells like a balloon, expanding until it is stopped by the too-tight band of his undies.

The woman, undeterred, reaches up with both hands, slides her fingers under the fabric, and yanks down. Six inches of thick, meaty cock – nearly as wide as my wrist – flops into view, trapping the underwear against the balls and the shaft. My jaw drops at not only the width, but the shape of the head; a spherical tip covered with short, pointed barbs jutting in every direction. It reminds me of a sea urchin, albeit with much shorter spines.

I'm unable to look away as the woman pulls herself between the shark man's legs, spins around, and stands up in one fluidic move. She shimmies her body against his, tits exactly where his cock hangs, and he throws his head back and hisses through a mouthful of sharp triangular teeth.

He grabs and spins her around roughly, pressing his front to her back. Bending his knees, he wraps both hands around her cinched waist and lifts. I expect her to look upset or surprised by the manhandling, but instead, she looks satisfied, like the cat who ate the canary whole. Spreading her legs wide, she hikes up her short skirt and reveals her bare and glistening puss to the room.

VJ creams as the shark creature slowly impale himself in her in full view of the dance floor, the pulse of want and lust racing through me like an electric current. I know I should look away. I can't; I'm too captivated by the look of rapture crossing their faces as his massively spiked head disappears inside her considerably smaller quim with nothing but a mangled groan of satisfaction from her.

She looks so strong like she's in charge even though he's in control. I can't help but admire her confidence. It's something I've always wanted for myself but could never quite emulate.

VJ wordlessly demands we sample both beings before the night is over, but I'm less confident. Women have often filtered into my fantasies and daydreams, but after all the therapy I've had, fear of my mother has often been projected onto the women around me, making them far too intimidating and complicated to even consider approaching. As if she can hear my thoughts, the blue woman opens her eyes and catches me peeking. My cheeks heat and I quickly avert my gaze, hoping against hope she doesn't notice, but glance back a few heartbeats later to check.

She waits, her dark and mesmerizing gaze catching mine and holding it fast. This time, I can't look away, the inviting look on her face intoxicating. She raises her arms, fingers wiggling for me to join her, all while continuing to pump her hips against the thick cock lodged inside of her.

VJ whimpers, already picturing the soft press of her lips against our clit while the shark god shoves himself inside, barbs and all. Slick coats our inner walls in preparation for his inevitable penetration, and all I want to do is throw myself at both their feet and beg them to take me right there on the spot.

How will her lips feel against me, I wonder. *What will it be like to kiss a woman for the first time? Will it be soft and sweet, like Hermes, or will she devour me whole?* The questions tear through me, mounting and multiplying at overwhelming speeds, transforming my lust into anxiety, then a very real fear. *She won't like how I kiss,* my doubts whisper. *She'll be able to tell right away what a fraud I am. I mean... I have no idea how to go down on a woman!*

I shake my head, trying to clear the doubts away, and become aware of something rubbing into the soft curve of my ass. Turning my head, I come face-to-face with the same stag-headed man who bumped me earlier, using my distraction to start grinding up against me. I gape at him, appalled by how brazenly he's acting.

Suddenly it becomes too much all at once. The sound, the noise, the proximity, the sex... It's stimuli I tend to take one at a time, never all at once. My skin feels hot and tight, and my breath is coming in sharp pants. Between my legs, VJ throbs and pulses with pleasure and need, and even my nipples feel sore and achy.

Twisting out of his grip, I turn for the bathroom door but have lost all sense of where it is amidst the writhing dancers. The stag-man approaches, a look of concern on his face, but I quickly back away, only to collide with a dancer. Turning, I try to offer apologies to the being hit, only to be shoved in a different direction, then another, until I'm a pinball bouncing off flesh of all different shapes and sizes. By the time I finally spot a break in the crowd to escape through, I'm completely mortified.

So much for the brave new Delilah, VJ taunts as I flee.

Tears spring to my eyes, her comment hitting home, but I blink them back and continue to weave through the crowd, searching for a place to collect myself. I'm devolving in real-time, my introverted nature causing the small mote of confidence I'd created for myself in Duat to shrivel up and blow away.

I search for safe harbor, but everywhere I turn,

Mona Ventress

I'm surrounded by mythological creatures from air, land, and sea, many engaged in sexual acts with each other. It all adds to the desperate throb between my legs, heightening my need to flee. *I want to come so badly,* I think. *But I can't do it like this! Not out here!*

I break free of the dance floor and the space opens into a shadowy sitting area, with furniture of all shapes and sizes strewn haphazardly around the room. Tables filled with more mythological beings take up the forefront of the space, and many sit in groups of similar-looking beings, creating cliques that remind me of high school. Empty glasses with melting ice crowd surfaces in desperate need of busing. I catch glimpses of short goat men wearing white tuxedo jackets racing around with trays, collecting dirty dishes, and delivering new beverages in a flurry of movement almost too fast for my eyes to track.

Rubbing my sweaty palms over the soft fabric of Hermes' dress, I search for an area devoid of life so I can catch my breath and calm down. In one direction, I'm blocked by a tall table surrounded by female centaurs, the height and breadth of their lower bodies too intimidating to try and navigate around.

Scanning, I discover two men with massive bull's heads blocking another path forward, aggressively making out while rubbing their crotches together. The tips of their massive cocks swell up and spill out over the matching tight short shorts they're wearing, and I can't help but stare at the smooth heads larger than my fist, rubbing against each other, strands of precum continuing to connect them when they pull apart. VJ drools, aching to be caught between them with dicks spreading both holes wide, and it takes every ounce of willpower I have to look away.

My third and final option turns out to be the best, featuring a naked fairy with blue hair and wings, tied spread-eagle on an otherwise empty table. She writhes in her bonds, hips un-dulating in a blatant invitation, but surprisingly, there's no one around. I don't second guess it, beelining towards her as hopes of a secluded spot deeper in the club begin to fill my mind.

I begin to slide past, already eyeing a tantalizing shadowy alcove just past another row of tables, when the woman seizes violently, arms and legs beating a staccato rhythm against the tabletop. I freeze and risk a glance over.

"*Nnnnng!*" Her eyes meet mine over a ball gag in her mouth for a brief instant before rolling into the back of her skull. She goes limp.

My eyes go wide, and I'm torn between concern and running. Looking around, I realize no one is paying attention to either of us and know I can't leave until I'm sure she's all right. Taking a step toward her, I stretch out my hands but hesitate, unsure of how to help. *The gag, maybe? Or should I check her pulse first?*

A small shadow darts over her breast in a flash so fast that I almost believe I've imagined it. Blinking, I stare at her skin, searching for any sign of life, when another shadow darts by, followed by a third one, both heading in the same direction. Lowering my face closer to inspect, I grow concerned she might be infested with insects or something when one of them stops moving at her navel.

My eyebrows come together, and I lean in until my nose is almost touching her belly, unable to tear my eyes away from the two-inch tall human perched next to her belly button. I make out basic details of two arms, brown hair collected in a ponytail, pale green eyes, and a tiny, flopping penis between two legs before he blurs into motion, streaking toward her erect nipples.

I blink rapidly, trying to clear my vision, but can't make the dozens of tiny people surrounding her nipples, using silver piercings lancing through the dark tips to twist them into tight little points, go away. I hear a little shout come from between her legs and follow the sound down to find even more of them using the folds and pubic hair around her pussy as holds to manipulate her cunt and clit. VJ clenches as a sopping wet man slips out of her opening, glistening from head to toe in her juices, and starts undulating in desire.

The man wipes his face and gasps for air, before peering up at me.

"Are you wantin' a turn then, love?" he shouts, his distinctly Irish lilt barely audible over the sounds of the club around me.

Yes, VJ whimpers, thrusting our hips forward so she can be a little bit closer. *All their tiny little mouths licking and stimulating our clit, some spelunking deep inside while the others play with my nipples.*

My hips shift back and forth, the demand from between my legs threatening to override all reason. The man stares at me, clearly waiting for an answer. Slowly, my chin lifts, preparing to drop my head down in a nod.

Oh god – what am I thinking? I can't do this!

I turn and flee for the shadowy corner I spotted earlier. With every step, VJ grows more apoplectic, pulsing in protest while projecting graphic images of everything I had just denied us. I gasp as she replays the fantasy of the blue woman licking my clit while her shark-headed lover thrusts his barbed cock deep inside, knees buckling from the rush of lust tearing through me, and almost fall.

I catch myself and barely make it to the alcove before my hands slide between my thighs. Turning around, I back up as far as I can go into its shadowy recess, not stopping until my back hits the wall. The sound of my breathing is raw and ragged in my ears. My skin's flushed and sweaty. I can't stop picturing being locked in positions with all the creatures I've just seen. I want to be stuffed and toyed with, to know what it feels like to be on display in front of everyone while I come undone.

Yet here you are, hiding, VJ snarls. *Denying me of everything I deserve!*

I cup my throbbing sex through Hemes' dress. I know I should be ashamed or embarrassed, but all I can think about is releasing the relentless pressure pounding between them.

Thrusting my hips forward, I'm speared on the shark man's cock. Back, the blue woman presses her face between my thighs, tongue flicking rapidly against my clit. Forward, my nipples tingling as the little men massage and knead them. Back, tilting my head up to Hermes, his lips pressing against mine in a sweet and gentle kiss, just like he did in the bathroom.

I orgasm so intensely; the effect is blinding. A low moan slips past my lips but is lost against the pulsing music. My body convulses, muscles spasming as I lose control. I lock my knees upright, but for several moments, I am lost to everything save for the waves of pleasure exploding through me.

Eventually, the blood and endorphins clouding my head recede, and my harsh breathing softens and evens out. Club music creeps back in, and my eyes snap open, suddenly remembering where I am. I look around, terrified someone has noticed my display, and am strangely disappointed when I realize no one has.

Maybe I am ready for this, I think as I catch my breath and continue to twitch. *Also… that fucking kiss! How could something so sweet and innocuous be such a huge turn-on? How can he?*

"Fuck," I exhale, shaking my head to clear my thoughts of Hermes and the perpetual war my mind and body are having over him. A cold sweat breaks out on my forehead and the back of my neck, helping cool my body and allowing my spine to reform. Straightening my back, I take in a cleansing lungful of air and subtly try to stretch my limbs to ease the spasms and twitches still echoing through my body. I can't believe I lost control like that! I can't believe I just masturbated in a club full of people, and nobody noticed.

"I did," a voice whispers behind me.

A scream escapes my throat, and I leap forward and spin automatically, praying I just imagined it. Instead, I find a tall man emerging from the shadows, his focus completely on me, and realize I had been leaning against him the entire time I masturbated. He'd seen everything. My eyes widen and I stagger back, cheeks going white-hot with mortification. "Oh god," I breathe, shaking my head in denial. "Oh no!" I search for an exit, muscles once again tensing to flee.

"Nuh-uh. None of that, poppet," he declares in a rich voice, words delivered in a distinctly Greek accent that make VJ quiver. I risk a glance at him and freeze, awestruck by the beauty of the being before me. Whereas I had doubted Hermes' status as a god when I first met him, I have no illusions about the creature in front of me.

He wears an extremely short toga, revealing muscular thighs that lead to shapely calves bulging through the laces of his Roman-style sandals. Brown wavy hair falls over his shoulders, some of it mingling with the dark springy curls coating his chest. The beard covering his chin is thick and well-trimmed, making his very pink and glossy lips stand out.

My gaze climbs up over his angular nose, too curious to be stopped, but freezes when I catch his eyes, the rich green, brown, and gold forming an ancient forest caught in the hazy dusk of sunset. I feel a pull in my stomach urging me to climb into them and lose myself in the wildness beyond, and it leaves my heart, lungs, and quim gasping with want.

Mona Ventress

Luckily, I'm distracted by the lights shifting, illuminating glittery rainbow eyeshadow that dominates the upper half of his face. The look is completed with an audaciously winged gold eyeliner and lashes so long they had to be fake. It's breath-taking and gorgeous, and all I can do to keep from spreading myself open in complete supplication.

I shudder as he takes a step toward me, hooking a knuckle under my chin and lifting it up so he can peer directly into my eyes.

"Tsk, tsk," he croons in a rich voice that rides the line between masculine and feminine. "Coming without a friend in Nimble is a cardinal offense and must be punished."

It takes a second for what he says to register in my ears. "Wait, I can explain!"

He chuckles and shakes his head. "They always try, but it doesn't matter. My club, my show, my rules." With that, he snaps his fingers, and a wave of inky black shadows explode from behind him and gobble us up.

Chapter Five

Light returns a second later, like I've just blinked, but the location has completely changed. The immediate area is dark and gloomy, yet the same music from the club continues to blare, though the source of it has shifted to the left and is considerably muted. A glance in that direction reveals I'm thirty feet behind the DJ booth, buried in a shadowy alcove.

"Hello?" I call, turning around and searching for any sign of movement.

"*Shh!*"

I leap and spin at the unexpected sound, combing the dim area for the source. My eyes study the shadows for any hint of movement or shape, when a blue light blossoms, making my pupils constrict painfully. I close my eyelids tight, giving them a second to adjust.

Mona Ventress

When I finally re-open them, I find the man standing a few feet to my right, an orb emitting a dim blue light floating next to his head, illuminating his face while he checks his appearance in a compact mirror.

"Oh. Uh... Hi! I-I-I'm Delilah."

One thick eyebrow raises in the reflection. "Duh."

I flinch, shoulders hunching as my self-consciousness grows, but I can't stop - the urge to know what happens next is too strong to resist.

"Right. Um... well..." I clear my throat. "I'm sorry for breaking your rules, or whatever, but I seriously didn't know. I was just overwhelmed by everything out there and I didn't know where you were..." I peer into the mirror, hoping for some sort of facial cue, but he just stares at me, eyebrow still up and judgmental. I suddenly realize I don't know if this is Bacchus or not. "Oh no. Are you even Bacchus? You must be him, right? I mean look at you! You're perfect and fabulous and..."

Shut up, a voice commands. *You're rambling!* I obey, all too aware I don't have the tools to explain how I came to be masturbating in his club in the first place.

Ask how he intends to punish us, VJ gleefully interjects, thoroughly excited by the prospect.

His mouth purses into a tight bud of disdain. "If you have to ask," he scoffs, eyes rolling in his skull for one revolution before turning the mirror back on himself.

A chorus of cackling laughter follows his dismissal, and I twist around to find three women standing in a semi-circle behind us, each one holding a tray covered with objects. The women are as different as the items on their trays, but glare at me like I'm a bug they desperately want to squash.

"She doesn't even recognize him," sneers an auburn-haired woman draped in a sapphire, ankle-length toga complementing orange skin and slitted green eyes. She circles me, one thick thigh jutting from a slit in her toga with each step she takes on her three-taloned feet. Her smooth flame-colored flesh is interrupted by obsidian ridges following the lines of her leg. Shifting a tray covered with make-up and brushes toward Bacchus, she raises one black eye ridge. "Do you wish us to kill her for this insult, Glorious One? I'll roast her alive for your supper if it pleases you." She huffs through her nose, causing two small jets of red flame to burst from her nostrils in a blast of heat.

I take a healthy step back, the lethal promise in her voice ringing with sincerity.

"Now, now Eryth," chirps a willowy woman with rough brown skin and some sort of green afro wig framing her face. She balances a tray overflowing with fruit and cheese over one shoulder and wears a short creamy toga that barely comes a quarter of the way down her thighs, revealing long slender legs speckled with green fuzz.

It takes me a moment to realize it's moss, and that she's some sort of tree-woman, but when I do, I can't help but gape. "His Radiance clearly needs something from her, something we can't provide." The pain in her face and voice is palpable, but she puts it

51

aside to declare, "We must be strong. What pleases our lord must please us as well, even if it is a doughy human."

"Excuse me?" I say, arching an eyebrow. Coming after my body shape is a low and petty blow. "Listen here, you little tw – "

"Oh, it wants to pretend it has spirit."

A third woman emerges from the other side of Bacchus, and my breath catches in my throat at the violet goddess before me. A shimmering gold toga clings to glistening iridescent purple skin, leaving one breast exposed to the world, dark nipple and all. The sides of her head are shaved bald, but her hair is a dark burgundy, caught between red and plum, falling over one side of her face and shoulder in a perfect array of soft-looking waves. Black, nascent eyes search my own for a long moment, then glance away in disdain. "It's pathetic when inferior creatures try to be something other than they are."

A black tentacle reaches up and picks up a coppery goblet from the tray she balances on one hand, and I follow it down to find it – and several more – writhing in and out of the slit in her toga. "Are you some sort of squid-woman?"

The woman's dark eyes flick at me over the lip of the cup pressed to her mouth, but she drains it all before responding. "Octopus, you bipedal excuse for a primate." She tosses the empty cup behind one shoulder then squares up to me. "I've eaten fish cleverer than you."

The disgust and disdain in her voice are thick, but it only causes my spine to harden and my chin to lift. I don't like bullies, and I'll be damned if I'm going to let this one tear me down. I do that just fine on my own; I don't need her help. "You know, I forget the exact amount of octopus humans consume on a yearly average, but I think it's something around 400,000 metric tons? Pretty sure that makes me the one at the top of the food chain, so…" And in a move that surprises even me, I bare my teeth and bite the air between us twice in a blatant threat.

Eryth and Dahlia giggle, causing the octopus woman's cheeks to turn a very attractive scarlet. Her eyes narrow at me, a deep crimson blooming in the center of her chest and radiating out across her skin like a red alert. She glides toward me on a mass of roiling tentacles, and I take a step back, hands lifting in a defensive gesture.

"Alyxs, bring me a drink," Bacchus interrupts, snapping the compact closed and tossing it to Eryth. She catches it without so much as jostling a single item on her tray. "Dahlia, fetch me the microphone. Eryth, tell Death Roll this is the last song." The three women snap to attention and move in opposite directions.

Surprise ripples through me at how quickly they obey his orders. Even Alyxs practically trips over her tentacles to offer him her tray. Her malice is instantly forgotten and replaced with a rapturous look making her eyes glisten with an anime-like quality.

Bacchus snatches a goblet from the tray, lifts it toward me with a sly smile, and drains it even faster than Alyxs did earlier. Tossing it over his shoulder with a belch, he grabs two more. "Love that fire, darling," he says, pushing one into my hand. "Use this to keep it burning. You're going to need it."

My fingers close around the stem automatically, and I blink at him. "Why? What is it?"

"It's wine, of course," he says with a surprised laugh. "Don't they teach you anything these days?"

I open my mouth to apologize, cheeks flushing with embarrassment, but he waves it off and continues.

"Never mind all that – drink! I grow the grapes myself, you know. Harvested, fermented, and crafted with my own two hands for only the most... devoted of beings." One finger strokes over Alyxs' cheek and her eyelids flutter closed in a true bliss that makes me slightly uncomfortable.

He raises his cup to me and smiles expectantly, but it takes me a second to realize what he wants. "Oh!" I stare down at the goblet in my hands, instincts screaming at me to politely decline.

He's the god of wine, Delilah! There's no telling how strong this is going to be, and you haven't had alcohol in forever. "I'm not so good with booze," I confess awkwardly.

Alyxs eyes snap open and Dahlia glares daggers at me as she walks up, a black microphone with a golden head in one hand. "Why are you playing with her," she whines to Bacchus as she hands him the mic. "She clearly has no respect or love for you, not as we do. Please, let me take her place tonight. I can please you so much better than she ever will. I mean, she's refusing a taste of what you made for her!"

Bacchus smiles and cups her cheek. "I know, pet, but you'll have to forgive our little human. She's lived with such prudes for so long that she doesn't know how to let loose and have fun. I'm sure my precious Maenads will help her remember, yes?"

I raise an eyebrow at the mixture of pain and adoration on her face, expecting her to protest, but she nods her head and smiles at me, all her earlier hatred simply... gone. "Of course, my Bliss," she intones.

The sudden shift in her attitude is so unnerving that it's almost a relief when I turn and find Alyxs right by my side, her smile one of a wolf baring its fangs. "You heard our lord," she says, one tentacle lifting and curling over my hip. "Drink up." Her dark tone promises violence if I refuse, and another tentacle wraps around my hand, pushing the cup toward my mouth. "Now."

I look to Bacchus for reassurance, but he just smirks and shrugs while stroking the ridges in Eryth's arm. "My Maenads adore everything about me, Delilah, and will destroy anyone who doesn't give me the satisfaction I desire."

"That's– " Alyxs shifts slightly like she senses what I'm about to say and is primed to attack, and I stop before I say 'crazy.' Both Anubis and Hermes' had warned me about the immaturity of the gods, and this exchange is proving their points. "When in Rome, right?" I say, lifting my glass to meet his with a metallic clang.

"To us."

Bacchus smiles and tosses back his drink in one smooth motion, Adam's apple bobbing with each long pull. I hesitate, glancing over at Alyxs. Her gaze is completely fixated on me, studying me like I'm a fish in a bowl she's planning to pluck out and eat. She doesn't relax until the rim of the cup is between my lips and I'm tilting it up, and even then, there's a disappointment in how her shoulders fall that tells me she had hoped I'd refuse.

The cool liquid hits my tongue in a wash of tart sweetness coating my mouth like a spoonful of honey, but with all the heating effects of alcohol. I swallow automatically, and the small sip carves a hot trail all the way down into my stomach, filling it with a warm and fuzzy light. Immediately, some of the tension leaves my body.

I open my eyes to find Bacchus giving me a knowing smile, but it disappears quickly as Eryth comes up behind him and whispers in his ear. Long eyelashes sweep up and down as he listens intently, nodding every so often. "Thank you, darling," he finally says, turning his face to hers and giving her a light peck on the mouth. She squeals and swoons, one willowy hand coming up to her forehead, but somehow manages to keep her tray perfectly balanced.

Bacchus chuckles and reaches up to his head, as if to adjust a hat he isn't wearing, and a bunch of leaves, vines, and grapes sprout from his fingertips and wrap together, forming a crown around his head. He wiggles it back and forth for a moment, nods as if satisfied, then plucks the microphone up from where it's floating beside him.

"Game faces, ladies. It's showtime." Bacchus claps his hands and the three women usher me away.

"What show?" I ask over my shoulder, but Dahlia simply says, "Shhhh," while Eryth pushes me forward, ignoring my question. *I thought it was just going to be an orgy! I'm supposed to perform something!?* I immediately look around, searching for the closest escape route, but Alyxs glides in front of me, cutting off any attempt.

"None of that," she declares, spinning me around to face Bacchus, his back now to us.

Her nails dig into my shoulders, holding me in place. Eryth and Dahlia take a position on either side of me, boxing me in. I quiver, muscles trapped between fight and flight, and try to breathe, but the feeling is dashed as the song ends and lights go out. A spotlight hums to life, illuminating Bacchus in a white-blue ethereal glow. The entire room bursts into applause.

"Thank you, thank you," Bacchus declares magnanimously, waving at the crowd. "And thank you for your continued patronage to Nimble, the only remaining bastion holding fast to the ideals of truth, liberty, and pursuit of sexual liberation!"

The crowd erupts in riotous cheers and catcalls, but I quickly tune it out, stomach and heart sinking into my feet. *I'm really going to fuck him on stage,* I think, panic building. *I know I thought I could handle this, but I was wrong! There are so many people out there; they'll be grossed out when they see how fat I am. They'll hate the sounds I make! I'll bore them to tears with my inexperience!*

"If you try to run, I will hunt you down and ram my tentacles so far up your cunt that you'll be ripped in half," Alyxs whispers in my ear, as if she can sense my mounting panic. My skin crawls as something cold wraps around my ankle, and I turn my head to find her face inches away from my own. "You don't want to disappoint my love, do you?"

Her voice is tinged with an underlying eagerness like she's hoping I'll run despite her graphically violent threat. The tentacle around my leg surges up to my knee and – despite the queasiness in my stomach – VJ rises from her briefly satisfied state with a vengeance, picturing Alyxs pinning us to a wall and using four tentacles to hold us down and spread us wide, while the others begin to probe –

Stop it, I think at her, cutting off the fantasy before it can go any further. *She wants to kill me!* I realize I need to get Alyxs' attention off me, so I bare my teeth in the facsimile of a smile and hold up the metal goblet before draining it in two long pulls.

The sweet cloying liquid inside hits my tongue and pours down my throat like a hot honey bomb, burning a path straight down and lighting my gut up like a Christmas tree. A warm glow follows quickly, spreading outward and leaving me tingling and significantly more relaxed.

I decide I don't hate the wine, especially since one cup already has me forgetting my stage fright.

Maybe this won't be so bad, I reason internally. *I'm different now. I stood up to Jason, so nothing is holding me back. Besides, I've had fantasies about being watched. This is my chance to finally see if it's all I imagined it to be, right?*

I wince at the small voice of doubt turning my declaration into a question and swipe another glass off Alyxs' tray and down it too, drowning them out. A second wave of heat races through me, so intense that sweat instantly beads on my chest, neck, and forehead. Even more of the tension leaves my body, eased away by the liquid warmth of my bloodstream.

"Don't think I'm impressed," Alyxs growls in my ear. "You'll never be able to give him what I can." Her gaze drifts towards Bacchus, adoration clear on her face. "I have satisfied my lord for decades, far longer than Dahlia and Eryth have even been alive, let alone his Maenad. I know exactly how to please him. Exactly where he craves to be touched. Exactly how to give him what he needs." Her voice becomes a menacing purr as her tentacle tightens on my thigh to emphasize each word. "No mortal woman could ever compare to me."

I blink several times, brows furrowing in confusion. *Why would she go out of her way to even say that,* I find myself wondering. *Of course I can't compare! She's a violet goddess, perfect in shape and form. I'm a drab field mouse compared to her.* I twist my head toward her, trying to read her expression, but she ignores me in favor of Bacchus, staring at him like he's the sun and moon of her world.

VJ ignores my confused suspicion, choosing to

focus instead on the placement of her tentacle in conjunction with my quivering quim. It feels only millimeters away, making me jerk and twitch in anticipation of their inevitable penetration, even despite the vitriol she's displaying toward me.

We're so close, VJ whimpers, and I realize she's right. We're hovering on the edge of orgasm, despite the alcohol coursing through my body. *Or maybe because of it?*

I look down at the cup in my hand and realize I'm weaving back and forth. "Oh my," I exclaim. "This is potent stuff, huh? What proof is this?" I toss the empty cup over my shoulder and snatch another one from Alyxs' tray before she can stop me.

"She's too weak for him," Eryth declares in a low voice, ignoring my question. "How can she please him if she cannot handle such a small taste? We should do something!"

"It is not for us to question him," Dahlia replies, eyes wide and bright. "He has something special in mind for the human. Something she can give him that we can't."

"There is nothing she can give that we can't," Alyxs declares, tentacle flexing. I fight the urge to relinquish my weight to her, to work one the invasive appendage closer to my cunt, but dimly realize attracting her attention right now might not be the wisest idea. "Clearly, she's going to be some sort of sacrifice, or maybe an offering to another deity our lord wishes to have at his party.

"Or maybe he's just tired of being surrounded by such catty bitches," I drunkenly interject. "I mean, seriously ladies! It's the modern era of feminism and all you're trying to do is tear down another woman because what? Your man wants to sleep with 'em? Whose fault is that, really? Mine or – "

"Shut up, shut up!" Alyxs shakes me through my arm so violently that my head bobs back and forth. "Of course it's your fault you stupid bitch! If you hadn't – "

She stops mid-sentence as a bright spotlight suddenly shines on both of us, and Bacchus' voice declares, "That's right, ladies and gentle beasts! For tonight, I have a special guest to inspire tonight's festivities – a human, from the mortal world!" *Ohs* and *ahs* follow his declaration. He gives them a beat before adding, "A human, barely touched by us so-called mythological creatures, will be my co-star in tonight's theatrical rendition of Temptress Punished."

Alyxs' face pales, her eyes widening in real terror, but I lose sight of it a heartbeat later when the other two Maenads give me a hard shove. Then I'm stumbling into the raucous applause of the stage beyond, completely unprepared.

Chapter Six

$\mathcal{B}$acchus hooks me around the waist before I fall and spins me in a full circle. "Isn't she graceful, folks?" he declares in the microphone, encouraging a chorus of laughter from the crowd.

My cheeks heat, the weight of dozens – if not hundreds of eyes – becoming a visceral weight on my exposed skin. I want to cover up, to hide and run backstage, but as I look over my shoulder, I see the Maenads spreading out, ready to catch me. Alyxs meets my gaze with a glare of pure hatred, and I know in my heart that she'll tear me apart if I run and she catches me.

She won't hurt me, I try to reassure myself. *She can't! She may hate me for some reason, but it doesn't matter. Hermes is out there, watching. He'll make sure nothing happens to me.*

The hope belongs to the thirteen-year-old me who still believes in knights in shining armor. Even still, I'm still bolstered by the thought, spine stiffening and stance widening. I search the crowd for just a flash of his springy gold curls or Mediterranean eyes. The house lights are completely down, making the crowd an indiscernible grouping of shadows.

Bacchus releases me and struts across the stage on a pair of glittery red heels he must've magicked on himself when I wasn't looking. Twirling on a leg, he stops himself with a loud *thwack* on the stage floor and poses theatrically. He flourishes with one hand as a stack of announcer cards appears between his fingers. Squinting at them, he plucks a pair of wire frame glasses from thin air, eliciting another chuckle from the audience, and reads: "Our heroine tonight is a thirty-year-old freelance accountant from Earth, recently resurrected and looking to party. Luckily for her, she broke a cardinal rule at Nimble: Orgasms must always be shared with a friend."

He pauses as a collection of *boos* and *sss* fill the room – not as thunderous as the applause – but loud enough that my confidence bleeds away. I look down at the stage, trying to memorize the patterns on the floorboards.

This is all your fault, I glower at VJ.

Her response is a slow liquid throb that takes me back to that moment, hidden in the alcove with my hand between my thighs, but now with the knowledge I was pressed against him the entire time. Warmth washes through me as my adrenaline spikes. Suddenly, I'm horny all over again.

I risk a glance over at Bacchus only to find him waiting for me, smirking knowingly. It occurs to me that he can read my mind like Hermes can, and the heat in my face bursts into full-on flames as waves of humiliation lance through me. I blink away tears, hoping no one notices, and pray for the horror show to end.

He turns to the crowd, hands spreading wide to stop their grumbling. "Now, now. This is not her fault. We all know the mortal world is really to blame! First by repressing people until they lash out abusively, then by shaming them for having perfectly healthy sexual desires. I mean, how many of us haven't fantasized about being taken by a minotaur or held captive by a gorgon? How many of us want to be railed by a gargoyle, or be given as a gift to a vampire prince? I know I certainly do – and have. Hey Dracula, so good to see you again!" He waggles his fingers in a direction, and I immediately follow it, eyes wide and heart pounding.

Dracula's real?! And here?! I try to follow the direction of his fingers, but once again can't see anything past the glaring lights.

The crowd laughs good-naturedly as Bacchus continues. "Delilah is no different than any of us and deserves to break free from the imposed shame those puritanical humans force on each other, wouldn't you agree?" He pauses long enough for the crowd to assertively shout their concurrence. "And shouldn't we, beautiful and exquisitely generous Bacchae, be the ones to introduce her to that freedom?"

Mona Ventress

Ecstatic screams answer his question, the voluminous roar of the crowd's abject approval deafening. I try to swallow the hard lump of panic forming, but my throat and mouth are too dry. My heart slows to a crawl, threatening to give out. This was going to be so much easier when it was just an orgy, I lament, panic rising.

Knowing there's nowhere to run, I spot the goblet in my hand and swallow down a mouthful, needing the liquid courage. The sugary alcohol wets my tongue, dissolves the knot in my throat, and carves a tunnel through my anxiety, allowing me to breathe a little easier. Even still, it does little to diminish the terror bubbling in my gut.

I keep repeating Hermes' words, telling myself I can leave now I know what Bacchus wants from me, but something keeps me from doing it. A part of me knows it's because I have a deep-seated desire to please others, and the thought of disappointing Hermes before I even try is worse than the potential humiliation of being onstage. Another tells me I need to stay for myself, so I can finally grow into the brave, confident human I've always wanted to be. Both aren't wrong.

I want to be here. To see if I can handle what the gods have to offer, to learn about my desires and separate fantasy from reality. To reaffirm the life I've reclaimed after standing up to Jason, to feel it connected with another being and know I'm alive and whole. To test if I'm truly free from the past version of myself and capable of enjoying myself without my traumatic past haunting me.

Not to mention, it's been so long since I've felt sexy or desirable. Hermes makes me feel all that and more. He makes me feel wanted. *He makes me feel like I have so much to offer. Supports me exploring my sexuality freely and earnestly, without prejudice. Even knowing he's out there watching sends a thrill down my spine. I've never felt so encouraged by another person. It's honestly a nice change of pace.*

Bacchus moves into my periphery, still speaking into the mic, and I realize I've zoned out and missed everything he's saying. I tune back in just in time to hear: "That's why, ladies and gentle beasts, tonight's show will be a double feature in more than one way. As punishment for her transgression, she must now share her orgasms with not one, but two of us! That's right – one of you will audition to be our third in *Temptress Punished*, right here, on this very stage."

Surprise ripples through me followed by understanding. *That's what Hermes meant by getting to join us.* VJ pulses with a beat of a war drum which echoes the steady thrumming of my heart with each jeer and encouraging hoot from the crowd. *But if Bacchus is opening it up for auditions... then there's a chance he won't join us. I mean, I would pick him in a heartbeat, but something tells me that Bacchus gets the final say.*

Then who? VJ immediately flashes us back, rolling through the litany of creatures we'd encountered in the club, and I close my eyes against the litany of lust rushing through me.

That shark creature would tear us apart, I reason.

67

Mona Ventress

And I don't think I could keep it together if those tiny Lilliputian-looking fuckers were crawling over me. I'd probably wind up laughing so hard that I'd accidentally crush a few of them... Oh my god, how awful would that be?!

Or how amazing they would feel, VJ counters, flexing walls growing slicker.

What about Hermes, I argue. *What about–*

Suddenly he's over me, watching as Bacchus thrusts and the shark god bites at my tit. Hermes' shoulder moves, and I follow his arm down to find his hand gripped tight over a thick, meaty cock that pulsates and twitches seconds before spurting, his hot jizz splattering on my neck and chest, aquatic eyes glistening with pride and want.

I lift the cup and chug the contents, trying to cool blood threatening to boil out of my skin.

Mistake.

The resulting alcoholic bomb hits me like a ton of bricks, making my bones and muscles dissolve. The world weaves around me, as if it's dancing. I lift my arms to join it with a delighted giggle. I know I'm making a spectacle of myself, but VJ's insistent demands are lessened. I can breathe again.

"Uh-oh," Bacchus croons in my ear. I jerk upright like a soldier called to attention. Peeling open heavy eyelids, I discover his arm wrapped around my waist, holding me up. "Looks like our precocious little human can't handle how potent I – I mean, the wine – is."

The crowd roars at the innuendo in his tone. "Sorry," I mumble. I wince at how slurred I sound but can't stop the words from coming out. "I don't drink a lot these days and this is just... strong." I break off, shaking my head and working my jaw back and forth. "Something's wrong with my mouth."

"Mmm... nothing's wrong with your mouth, baby girl," Bacchus replies, stepping in close enough behind me until I'm leaning on him. I'm grateful for the support, as it helps the room stop moving back and forth. "You're just drunk on me."

I giggle. "'Cause you're the god of wine," I manage to work past my malfunctioning jaw. The sensation makes me laugh harder, and I tip forward, losing all strength in my spine.

Bacchus catches me before I go too far, pulling me back against his chest. "It seems our heroine needs a moment to collect herself before we begin the scene."

"Put her in the shower," Alyxs shouts from backstage. "She smells like wet dog."

I hunch my shoulders. *I knew a magical cleaning wouldn't be as good as a shower,* I think.

"Pay her no mind, pet," he breathes in my ear, hands sliding from my waist to my breasts. "Hermes did a good job cleaning you." His fingers find and pinch my nipples hard enough to make me gasp. VJ responds violently, jerking forward – already warm, wet, and ravenous – then forcing our hips back, rolling my soft ass against his hard front.

Bacchus groans and grinds back for a long moment before letting go. "As much as I would enjoy spreading you open in front of my guests, I promised one would be lucky enough to play with you too, and I'm nothing if not true to my word."

I pout. "So, then… What do I do now?" I ask, turning around.

I stumble over the hem of my skirt and almost fall, but he holds me steady. "Even though Alyxs' suggestion was made maliciously, I do think a shower will clear your head," he replies. I open my mouth to object, but he continues, oblivious. "And it will give me time to consider the applicants for our third."

"No, wait! Can't I – "

I want to ask him if I can be involved – even despite the anxiety it creates – but Bacchus snaps his fingers and the shadows once again gobble me up.

I appear in a shower stall approximately the size of my bathroom, completely alone. Spinning around, I search for a door, ready to march back out through the club to demand inclusion in the decision-making process. I only find four walls covered with mottled brown tiles, one of which bears familiar silver fixtures.

As soon as I notice them, they rotate under some invisible force, releasing an icy torrent of water from above. Shrieking, I leap out of the way and press against a wall, shrinking back from the frigid droplets. I reach for my dress, not wanting it to get ruined under the water, only to find myself naked yet again.

"Again? Seriously? What do you assholes have against clothes?!" I pause, waiting for a response, then add, "And I better get that dress back!" *Hermes made it for me.*

I don't add the last part, but there's a pang of longing in my chest that accompanies the idea of losing it, and I resolve to ask Bacchus about it as soon as he lets me out. Whenever that might be.

Hugging myself, I rub my arms to try and retain some of the precious warmth Bacchus' wine infused me with. It doesn't work. The cold tiles at my back steal the heat from my very bones, replacing it with cold knives that slice deep into the marrow. It isn't too long before my teeth are chattering together.

I look around, searching for some sign of what I'm supposed to do through bleary and drunk eyes when I notice wisps of steam forming around the overhead cascade, tendrils beckoning. Sticking my hand into it, palm up, I find the stream quickly passing body temperature. I quickly step under the spray. Blowing out a shaky breath, I tilt my face into the water, letting it wash away the alcohol and center myself.

The water is magic on my skin, rivulets dripping over my eyes and wetting my hair. I know it'll be a mess later without any products, but for now, the feeling is close to orgasmic. *Alyxs is a crazy bitch,* I think, *but this is exquisite, so... gonna go ahead and call this a win for me.*

A smile blossoms on my face and a chuckle escapes me. I'm tipsy, but it's making me feel confident in a way that I desperately need, even if I haven't quite earned it yet.

Haven't I, my cantankerous side demands.

I lift my chin. "Yeah, haven't I?" I echo out loud. "I died and confronted my ex, bitch, then let the Egyptian god of death fuck my ass good. Pretty sure that makes me a badass!"

I snort out a laugh and stumble back a few steps, back slapping wetly against the wall, and laugh hard. "I'm such a dumbass! I'm talking to myself, trying to convince myself I deserve to be confident! That's… so…" I'm heaving too hard to come up with the right word, so I press my lips together and blow a loud raspberry.

"*Pbbbbbthththth!*" The subsequent sound has me laughing so hard that tears leak from my eyes. I slide down the wall before I fall, knees incapable of supporting my weight anymore. "Oh girl, we are waaaaasted," I declare, slapping my hands on the floor and creating a little splash.

I sit there for several beats, letting the fit of laughter subside and finally calm, then stare at my feet, trying to stop the world from gliding left and right by focusing on my exposed toes. It helps somewhat, but it isn't enough. My skin feels too tight and my stomach churns, angry I put such sugary alcohol in it over food.

Don't forget about me, VJ interjects, clenching in outright protest. *If you had just chilled out and maintained a little self-control, Bacchus might have let us participate in the choosing process. Now, we have no idea who we're going to get! I swear, if I am not stuffed with a huge cock by the end of the night, I will implode and kill us both.*

I roll my eyes at her antics but sigh heavily, the spirit of her message received. "I promise I'll stop freaking out about things and just try to relax, okay?" I'm not entirely certain I can back up that promise, but it's enough to assuage her. For now.

Settling back, I let the temperature difference between the water and tiles work to sober me up and close my eyes. I'm grateful for the privacy and silence but am unable to stop thinking about what Bacchus is going to do to punish me.

Maybe it's going to be some sort of BDSM thing? Maybe he'll have me tied up, with my arms over my head and just enough slack that my toes barely touch the floor?

My breath catches in my lungs as the fantasy unfolds, cutting through the alcoholic haze. VJ clenches in response, and the intensity of it has me gasping hard enough that my back arches and eyes burst open.

Hermes's hard, thick shaft impales me oh-so-perfectly, his hands holding my weight and keeping me upright. Fingertips dig into the flesh of my hips as he pumps in and out, in a long, slow rhythm, eyes holding mine. Behind me, Bacchus presses the blunt tip of his head against the tight ring of my asshole, and muscles retract, trying to ease his way.

I bite my lip, the temptation to reach between my legs and rub another one out is tantalizing. Hard to resist. *Could I get off before Bacchus comes back? How long does it take to pick a third, and what sort of trouble*

Mona Ventress

would I be in if he caught me?

A part of me wants to find out, another part urges caution, reminding me that the last time I masturbated, I got in trouble. In my drunken state, I'm too lazy to pick between the two.

Hermes takes a nipple in his mouth, gaze holding mine. I gasp, arching my back into him, and Bacchus uses the opportunity to slide the tip of his dick into my ass. My entry muscles throb around Hermes' perfect cock, and I cry out as I slowly begin to ride them both.

My hips shift and twitch from the force of VJ's need, and my hand drifts down my front, lazily heading for the apex of my thighs. *I'll just press on my clit a little,* I vow. *Just to relieve a bit of pressure. I won't come. I promise.*

I know I'm lying but can't stop, fingers already gliding over my pubic hair and dipping into my slit. I groan at the fluttering pleasure my fingers leave in their wake as I trace the wet folds around my entrance. *I'm closer than I thought,* I realize, clit and labia throbbing. *So very, very close.* I bite my lip, and keep my touch light, but know I'm fighting a losing battle.

A strange grinding sound fills my ears, and I snatch my hand back in alarm, eyelids popping open and looking for Bacchus. Blinking through the water droplets clinging to my eyelashes, I sit up, ready to meet him, but am still alone.

However, the sound persists, and I lean forward, rubbing my burning eyelids to clear them and discover the source.

74

The shower stall is the same, all four walls still devoid of any door leading out. Nothing else seems out of place.

Placing a hand on the wall behind me, I brace against it and stagger to my feet, convinced perspective is the problem. Something soft presses against my palm, and I jerk away from the cool flat surface, revulsion crawling up my spine. A dark hole, slightly larger than a silver dollar, has appeared in the tile where my palm had been seconds before. It's perfectly shaped, which tells me it's man-made, but as to its purpose…

I lean closer, trying to peer through it. My eyeball is only inches away when something blue and shiny pushes through. I jerk back immediately, thoughts of a snake or worm fueling the speed in which I react, only to find more holes opening, more differently colored tubes pushing through them.

Whirling around, I realize each wall is now pockmarked with them, all at different heights and sizes, and all very phallic.

"Um, Bacchus," I call, nervously, shifting my weight back and forth from under the stream of water pouring down from above. "Can you please *bamf* me out of here? 'Cause there's definitely something weird going on in here."

The first shiny blue worm suddenly stiffens and swells up, pulling itself into a straight line and finishing in a mace-like design I instantly recognize from the club. *It's shark guy's dick.* My eyes go wide.

I spin around, watching as more poke through other holes in the wall, until I am surrounded by an array of cocks of all shapes and sizes.

"What am I supposed to do with this," I wonder, lightheaded with lust and confusion.

Oh, I don't know what you're doing, but I know what I'm gonna do, VJ answers, contracting muscles so deep that my eyes cross and knees go weak. *Which is thoroughly enjoying all these wonderful playthings.*

Chapter Seven

"You did a good job finding this one, brother." The moniker curdles in Bacchus' mouth, the only evidence of our long-soured relationship. "She really does have a certain… sparkle to her, doesn't she?"

I keep my gaze on Delilah but don't let the conversation falter, aware I'm being closely monitored. "You know I have nothing to do with how they're chosen, Bacchus. But yes, I agree. She certainly is something."

Almost as if she can hear us, she reaches out with her index finger and pokes at one of the members jutting through the wall. From my side, I can see the being attached to it – a male dryad from the yew family – throwing back his bushy head, eyes rolling at the unexpected pleasure of being touched – but from her side, she has no idea the entire audience watches.

Normally, such displays would turn me on – and this is certainly no exception – but I can't help the thread of jealousy stitching across my hearts.

The organs in question pound erratically in my chest, falling out of their normal syncopated rhythm, and I realize I'm holding my breath. Delilah prods the cock a second time, pulling it up and down like a lever, and the dryad writhes.

"She's going to choose him?" Bacchus whines. "Ugh. I'm going to be pulling splinters out of my ass for a week! I retract the compliment, Hermes. She clearly has no taste."

"Give her a second," I reply, certain her curiosity is too great to settle for the first dick presented to her. *Besides, she'd never choose him. Those coniferous spines at the base of his dick are too strange for her current palate.*

She reaches out again, and for one surprising second, I think she's going to prove me wrong. Then she bats at it like a cat, making it bob up and down, and laughter bubbles out of her chest. It isn't long before she's doubled over, her alcohol-ridden state making it difficult to remain upright.

I smile, inordinately pleased by the sound. In my observations of her, she hasn't had much cause to laugh in recent years – and in spite of it coming from Bacchus' wine – it warms me to know she is still capable.

She eventually stops and rights herself, and I can't help but admire the water dripping over her ample curves. Her dark eyes blink away droplets from the showerhead above, considering Bacchus' offerings, and my shaft swells at the hunger sharpening her features. *Will she look at me like that when our time comes?* My hearts skip another beat, already imagining such a thing, and I find myself itching to throw her over my shoulder and take her right now.

What is this hold she has over me?

I can't describe when or how it started, only that I watched her for days before I made my approach, which was far longer than I had ever spent observing a potential lover. Normally, I lurk just long enough to catch them alone to make the invitation, but with her…

I followed her around like a lost puppy, I think, still disgusted by my lack of control. *Like it was the beginning of creation, and I was a callow youth blinded by nothing more than swaying hips and an inviting pair of tits.*

Yet I couldn't help it, utterly beguiled from the moment I'd appeared and found her ranting at the television in response to some broadcast. Her thoughts had been so insightful and sarcastic, reminding me of when I frequented the political forums in ancient Rome or got drunk with the farmhands after harvest. Her mannerisms and what she believes are so much more nuanced, and I found myself wanting to be on the other side, asking questions and making comments just to see how her delicious mind responded. It was like she was having half of a conversation I hadn't known I'd been longing for until that moment.

Granted, I hadn't the slightest idea on how to keep up with her. I'd turned my back on the mortal realm for the past few centuries, bitter and angry over how easily humans had forsaken me for their new, simplified religions. Or worse - something as fantastical to me as I had been to them: Science.

It all started with Prometheus, I think angrily. *The titan's desire to protect his creations from the monsters his brother had crafted led him to steal fire from Olympus and sparked the human's thirst for technology and innovation. If he'd just left them alone, to serve and placate us as Zeus decreed, none of this would've happened.*

I realize immediately it's an unfair perspective of the situation. Humanity looked to us as parents to guide them through life, and we failed them. We met their hopes and problems with indifference, used and discarded them at our whims, and treated them as collateral damage in the wake of our petty disagreements. *No wonder they turned to something as reliable as science. It shields them from our inconsistencies.*

Then again, they continue to be every bit as inconsistent as us, from their history books to their politics to their interactions with each other. It's like they broke away from us in the hopes of something better but still inherited all our flaws anyway.

Yet Delilah remains strangely optimistic – like she still believes it can be fixed despite all the omens screaming otherwise. Even when she harbors no hope for her own happiness, she still believes it's possible for others.

That's what drew me to her in the first place and continues to hold my fascination even now. I never thought I could do better; humanity had decided who and what I was long ago. Yet I know if I told Delilah that, she would tell me not to let what they thought of me interfere with who I want to be and encourage me to change.

That gracefulness... that belief and understanding and acceptance... It's something I don't deserve, yet crave nonetheless. It's a beacon of sunshine breaking through the gloomy clouds surrounding my existence, reintroducing color and possibility to what has become a bleak monotony of empty loneliness and making her more precious to me. She has every right to turn her back on that hope, especially after her mother's and ex's abuse, not to mention the untimely death of her father. But in the face of such grief and pain, she doesn't.

Instead, she chooses to care. She believes in the ability to preserve, to find it within to recognize flaws and overcome – something I can't even see in myself, let alone them. And she acts upon this belief every day, even if it's only trying to find peace and happiness within her self-imposed isolation. She isn't perfect, and there are days where it seems easier to give up than keep going, but she kept fighting. She didn't quit searching for happiness.

I admire that. In all my eons on this planet, it had never occurred to me that I could – or even should – change. Yet she makes it seem so possible that I find myself wanting to try.

And then I almost fuck it all up by not giving her the full details of the exchange with Anubis. My hands ball into fists and my stomach clenches tight as guilt, disgust, and rage play a dangerous three-way tug of war. *She should've made me drop out,* I think. *I should do it anyway despite her asking me to stay.*

But you won't, a voice inside taunts, once again highlighting how truly selfish and unworthy I am of her. *You can't let her go, because you greedily want her for yourself, even if she doesn't want the same.*

The voice isn't wrong but it belongs to the old me. The one I'm trying to shed like a snake does with its skin. Instead, I'll let her go. I'll stand by her side while she explores herself and what she wants, and give her whatever she needs to be happy, even if it's not me. *That's how I become better, and while I hope it's good enough to be worthy of her, I'll accept it if I'm not. That's how I honor her and the precious forgiveness she showed me today.*

The fact that she didn't let me withdraw gives me hope I want to cling to, but I know one more mistake will harden her heart against me, and I couldn't blame her. She needs someone earnest and honest, whose intentions match their actions.

That's never been me. I'm every bit as inconsistent and thoughtless as the rest of my kind. I lazed out on my job escorting the dead to Tartarus over personal and petty pursuits, and my emotionality has been just as volatile as Zeus.' And there I am doing it all over again because I want her optimism and brightness to light up a life I have barely been living.

"So quiet. What thoughts rage in that golden head of yours, brother?"

Bacchus' voice jolts me from the depths of my thoughts, and I turn away from Delilah and meet my younger sibling's wild green eyes, keeping my features pleasantly neutral. I can already sense the trap he's trying to lay for me, all too aware he noticed my prolonged time in the bathroom. I need to make sure I don't seem to care more about her than I should.

Than I already do.

Bacchus sits on a wooden throne grow-ing directly from the stage. His magick causes the tree trunk to bend and contort around his form before resuming its natural growth and creating a green canopy above. The space is lit by small orbs fixed to the branches, illuminating him and his Maenads.

Two stand behind him, trays and posture ready to serve at the slightest hint of their lord's needs. The third is positioned between his legs, green leafy head bobbing up and down. I arch an eyebrow at that, recalling his splinter quip, but let it go a moment later, all too aware of Bacchus' proclivity for being a hypocrite.

Soft wet sucking sounds fill the alcove, but only we can hear it; to the audience, we are completely invisible, allowing us to be closer to the action without impeding anyone's view.

"Nothing. Just that I'm sure you'll find Delilah a fabulous addition to the show," I inform him coolly. Behind him, the violet Cecaelia's eyes flare with hatred at my declaration, but it disappears a heartbeat later, her face falling back into an aloof mask that reveals nothing. I know I should be concerned, but in truth, I feel sorry for Alyxs. She's the oldest of Bacchus' current batch of Maenads, and therefore knows his attention on her is waning. It's only a matter of time before the fickle god replaces her with someone new and she joins the throngs of former Maenads populating the club, forever on the outside looking in, cursed with the knowledge of what she once had and lost.

"Hmmm..." Bacchus regards me under long lashes, gaze glittering enigmatically. "What's going on with you? Are you smitten with our little kitten? I mean... you did spend forever with her in the bathroom. Were you giving her a little pregame before the big show?"

I knew it was coming, so it's easy to keep calm and deliver my practiced lie in an indifferent tone. "She was emotional after her resurrection and upset that Anubis had sent her here without clothing. I didn't want her fragile state to interfere with the show or cause her to back out prematurely, so I helped her compose herself."

"Mmhmm... But I might have enjoyed watching her run around, shamed by her nudity yet aroused by the delights of my club. Did you not think of that?" He narrows his eyes, and it's hard to keep calm under the heavy pressure of his mind against mine, cleaving for answers I do not want to surrender. For several seconds, we stare off, a silent mental war waging under the sloppy wet soundtrack his Maenad provides filling the tense air between us.

"You'll have to forgive me, brother," I grate out between clenched teeth when he doesn't relent. I'm all too aware he is strong enough to break me eventually – he still holds the worship of pretentious students and rich wine connoisseurs around the globe – so I need to distract him if I'm going to escape unscathed. "It's been over two centuries since the last mortal was selected and they barely made it past you before deciding to end their experience." I pause for a breath, and inspiration strikes. "I'm here to make sure you intend to send Delilah home after the conditions of your contract have been met."

Bacchus blinks in surprise, then grins slowly, and the relentless probing of his mind evaporates. Leaning back, he strokes the dryad's leaves, making them rustle, yet never breaking eye contact. The powerplay is as blatant as it is childish, and I resist the urge to roll my eyes and simply wait for the mad god's reply.

"I'm under no such obligations to do so. The rules of my realm are as bound to me as I am to my domains. If she freely chooses to stay and submit to me then I cannot make her leave. And if her performance tonight is as good as you promise, well…" He gives a little shrug of supposed innocence while saying, "Why shouldn't I let her know all her options?"

My chin raises. "She won't stay." I know in my bones it's true, but saying it aloud is a mistake, one I desperately wish I can take back even as it's leaving my lips. "She won't choose you."

His gaze narrows and his head tilts, regarding me with growing disdain. "Such confidence in a woman you barely know. How can you be so sure?"

I know he wants me to admit my improprieties, but I'm an Olympian god and therefore a practiced liar. "I'm not. What I am certain about is the rules of this arrangement, which stipulate that any interference with the peaceful transfer of our guest will ban you from future events for a period of one thousand years."

Bacchus snickers, shoulders swelling like ocean waters at the forefront of a storm. "Oh no, whatever will I do? I had to wait two hundred years for this one, and with the way humanity is going, humans willing to entertain us will dwindle until they're non-existent. With her, I'll be able to play with and entertain myself until she dies. What is the human life expectancy up to these days, anyway? A hundred – two hundred years? I bet I can extend it for a significant period, given the right magicks and rituals." His eyes glitter with amused malice, and I can tell he's waiting to see how I will react.

I exhale through my nose and shake my head. "Right. So, I'll have backup ready for when she invariably rejects that completely one-sided and insane offer."

I expect him to get angry, but he simply shrugs and tosses his dark brown curls over a shoulder. "We'll see. Now shoo. You're making me miss the show."

He leans to one side so he can peer around me, and I glance back to see Delilah trying to straddle a cock far too thick for her. I smile despite the outlandish proportions of the two, pleased by her growing confidence, then launch into the air, determined to get an escape plan together for her inevitable 'no.' Bacchus will lose his shit, and while he couldn't harm her physically, that agreement did not extend to his Maenads.

Sorry I can't be here like I promised, but it's for good reasons, I swear, I think at her, wishing I could project my thoughts into her mind. I won't though; she asked for privacy and she's going to get it. *Just try to have fun and trust I'm looking out for you in every way I can.*

I take off toward the ceiling before the doubts can present themselves again and teleport away, intent on finding her next suitors and enlisting their aid in her extraction. Hopefully, the brothers will feel up to jumping realms, but if they don't, I'll have to go to the Benefactor, something I really don't want to do.

Chapter Eight

*V*J turns us around slowly, taking time to marvel at the array of dicks coming through the walls. *It's like a garden of cocks blooming just for me,* she thinks, and delight pools in my stomach. I can't disagree with the analogy: The dicks are an array of colors, shapes, and sizes, all vibrant enough to rival any garden.

I pause as the one I batted at earlier withdraws, leaving an empty hole behind. I stare, wondering if I should try to peek through it again to see what's happening on the other side, but it's filled moments later, replaced by a corkscrew-shaped phallus as red as a cardinal's feather. It's at least ten inches, but the width is barely as wide as my pinkie. VJ and I reject it almost immediately, the thin thing too comical to be taken seriously.

Next to it is a shorter one that starts out wide but

grows thinner the further away from the wall it gets and is inset with spiraling ridges that reminds me of a unicorn's horn. Beside it, nearly a foot lower to the ground, a short, thick, purple monstrosity bulges from the wall, the shaft covered with red, quarter-sized lumps that look too much like pimples to be anywhere near enticing.

The following one, however, draws me like a moth to a flame. The shaft is covered with symmetrical bumps spiraling down its length, and wide enough that VJ is certain she would strain to take it, which makes us want it more. Heart racing, I reach out to touch it before I can stop myself, eager to know how it feels.

The skin is surprisingly rough, the texture of sandpaper scraping at my palm. What's worse, the muscle is as cold as a block of ice, making me shiver despite the hot steamy water still pouring from above. I pull my hand away and turn, VJ and I in complete agreement that, while the size and shape had been perfect, neither of us had any desire to be rubbed raw and numb at the same time.

This is kind of fun, I admit, continuing my slow perusal of the smorgasbord of dicks around me. *With the men stuck on the other side of the walls, I'm in complete control. I can use them however I want and they can't stop me.*

The thought fills me with a rush of power and lust so intense that my eyes close and toes curl, dozens of fantasies playing out in my head. VJ pushes them aside, reminding me I don't have to fantasize – I can take what I want – and a slow predatory smile forms on my lips, alcohol and newfound power combining to awaken something deep and primal inside.

My gaze stops on a tempting offering that makes my mouth and cunt drool, and I move closer to investigate. This cock is meaty – as thick as my wrist and at least seven inches long, sitting at the perfect height – and ripe for the taking. I want to taste it.

I touch it first, making sure it's safe, and shudder at the scalding heat emanating from the smooth surface. It's not velvety soft, like a human, but it isn't rough either, like the last dick I touched. If it wasn't for the shiny purple color, it would remind me of still-healing scar tissue, the flesh stretched tight over the muscle below.

I bite my lip and look up at the wall. *Can he see me?* I wonder. *Or does he just feel me?*

My heartbeat skips at either possibility, making VJ jump and buck with want. I reach between my legs and spread my lips, feeling my own slickness, worrying his size and lack of lubrication will be an issue. Unlike a human cock, it doesn't have a head, or even a hole for ejaculation I can notice, so doubt there will be any pre-cum to assist.

VJ doesn't care, already turning us around so we can straddle the massive schlong. The head splits my folds open wide, pressing against the edges of my quim and clit as I ease it inside. My knees shake and thighs burn, but I ignore them, too eager to be filled beyond capacity. Leaning forward, I try to wiggle the smooth head back and forth into my entrance, but it's too blunt.

Mona Ventress

I reach down and stretch my entrance until it burns, then push against it.

Tight skin strains against tight skin. Muscles pulse, trying to give way, but even with VJ's lubrication slickening his surface, the circumference is too wide for my overly ambitious hole.

We can do it, VJ insists, rocking back and forth like a car stuck in the mud. My entrance burns with the effort, and I fear the delicate flesh will rip long before I can accommodate him.

That, and the ravenous creature inside me hungers to the point of mindlessness. I make one more attempt, pushing my hips down against the meaty dick, then give up, a frustrated growl tearing from my lips.

Stepping away, I whirl around, looking for another option that will relieve the mounting pressure building between my thighs. *Too small, too big, too weird, too...*

My thoughts cut off as I double-take the last one, which has two phalli coming from the same hole and wriggling around in random directions. Images tear through me of what it would feel like to take both at the same time, but VJ rejects the option outright, still too salty from our experience with Anubis to allow anything but full, vaginal penetration during this encounter.

The bestial creature riding my skin twists, scanning frantically, then freezes, spotting the most intriguing possibility yet – a red and black-streaked, eight-inch-long dong as wide as my middle three fingers pressed together. VJ pulses in agreement that she could gobble it down easily, and we move, decision made.

Crossing under the shower spray, I blink away the water streaming into my eyes and take a closer look at my chosen dick. The tip is dramatically different from a human's, flattened, smoothed out, and curved, like a shallow spoon, but with ridged edges that create an interesting scalloped-looking texture. *What it will feel like inside of me?*

Like the others, I run my hand over it, and gasp as a thick, reddish-tinted gel seeps from the skin in response, covering my fingertips in a slick lube. I grip tight and glide it down, moaning as the member swells and pulses in my hand, forcing fluid into little bumps that run up and down the underside of the shaft.

My eyelashes flutter and hips jerk as I imagine them gliding against me inside, and I can't wait any longer. I turn and straddle his cock, position the wide, ridged head against my entrance, and slowly lower myself on it.

The tip slips inside me and I savor the rough edges dragging against my silky walls, creaming with pleasure. I pump down on him, taking him deeper, and cry out at the exquisite sensation of being filled by a real dick for the first time in ages. The hard bumps on the underside of his dick rub over my entrance, and my eyes cross and knees buckle. I almost slide off him, but somehow, I keep my legs firm enough to keep going.

"Yes," I groan, tilting my hips down and back. I run my hands over my tits and sides, feeling the ecstasy of the moment. "*Yes!*"

I'm so close, teetering on the precipice of orgasm. One or two more thrusts, and I'll be gone. I'm beyond ready. *All sex should be like this,* I think, tweaking my nipples and rotating my hips. *I feel so good, so free!*

The cock inside me jerks and twitches, and VJ pulses in response. *We're going to come together!* A surge of heat and lust fires through me, and I drive my hips back, hard enough that my ass slaps against the tile. *I wish the wall wasn't between us. That his hands were on my hips and taking over…*

The cold tile behind me disappears, and I gasp as several more inches of cock fill me all at once, slamming into the end of me hard enough to make me shout. Hands grab me exactly where I want and hold me in place while he jerks his cock in and out of me.

"Good girl," a voice rumbles behind me.

I look over my shoulder, eyes wide and jaw dropping. A creature with deep red skin towers over me, staring down at me with golden sclera surrounding Saturn-shaped pupils under hairless brows. My mouth goes dry as I take in the shiny black horns erupting from his head and curving inward, like a bull, so long and sharp they almost distract from a crown of thorns and fire.

Almost.

The image is haunting and oh-so-familiar, but one I never thought I'd interact with, even with agreeing to be a lover to the gods.

94

Devils aren't gods, are they? Oh, sweet mother of monkeys! It can't really be him. Can it? I swallow hard and look between my legs, hoping against all hope that I'm wrong. My stomach drops several inches at the cloven hooves braced a few inches behind my bare feet.

"Let it be known our pet human has delectable and deliciously naughty tastes," Bacchus' voice announces to my left. My head follows the sound to find him standing a few feet away, his body facing away with the microphone to his mouth. I look where he's facing to find the audience peering in at me, and my blood freezes. I've been on display the entire time.

"Why else would she choose the Lord of Darkness himself to join us? That's right, folks! Give it up for the third in tonight's performance: Lucifer, King of Hell."

The crowd bursts into applause, but I hear none of it, too shocked that the literal devil is still rooted deep inside me. VJ, however, doesn't care, hips already wriggling and writhing for the sweet release hanging inches away.

Lucifer responds by thrusting forward, sliding against my walls. "Oh god," I cry, hiding my face in my hands because I can't stop what is about to happen.

He freezes, grip tightening against my hips. "Surely we don't have to bring daddy dearest into this," he rumbles good-naturedly, but I hear a threatening thread weaving through his voice and decide not to do that again.

Panting, torn between shame and orgasm, I

cannot formulate a word to save myself, and VJ will not be denied. She thrashes against his grip, hips undulating and muscles clenching tight on him, trying to force him to move.

Lucifer chuckles and pulls himself back. And back, and back, and… My eyes roll into the back of my skull. My spine twitches and legs tremble. VJ clenches, preparing for the next and final thrust.

"None of that, Luci," Bacchus chides. "She doesn't get to come yet."

No, VJ cries, pulsing in disbelief. "No!" I echo, unable to believe it either.

"I remember, forest god," Lucifer replies, slipping completely from my aching and needy channel.

I cry out, unable to stop myself. "Please!" I slap a hand over my mouth a second later, but it's too late. Both men turn toward me.

"Aww, poor baby," Bacchus croons, reaching out and cupping one cheek. "We'll treat that greedy pussy to a climax soon."

Before I can respond, he turns back to the crowd and holds up the mic. "Get your drinks, cocks, cunts, and every sex organ in between ready folks, because the scene you've all been waiting for will begin in five minutes."

The crowd applauds and cheers as the stage lights go out. From the darkness, the Maenads surround and force me off stage. I walk on rubbery legs, clit throbbing, VJ sobbing, and a strange sense of numb mortification building under my skin.

Glancing back, I see Bacchus and Lucifer chatting, and can't help but wonder what they have planned for me next.

Chapter Nine

$\mathcal{T}$he Maenads guide me to a shadowy alcove stage right, illuminated by a small twinkling lantern emitting a soft blue glow, and begin toweling me dry.

I barely feel them, so shaken I'm unable to focus on anything save the sound of my heart pounding in my ears, caught between shame and lust. *I just fucked Satan with everyone watching,* repeats on a constant loop in my head, followed by variations of, *I have to fuck him again. With Bacchus. On stage. In front of everyone.*

I can't reconcile the waves of apprehension, want, fear, and need tearing through me, so I remain still while they clothe me, complying mindlessly when hands lightly encircle my wrists and pull, letting them guide me where they will. The sound of fabric dragging over skin fills my ears, but it's a light roar compared to the churning mill of my thoughts.

I almost came in the shower in front of all those people. Oh god, how ridiculous did I look? How did I sound?! They must think I'm so boring! I mean, how could they not?! They're so unique and have such interesting genitalia! I'm just a human – there's nothing special about me at all!

My internal monologue is cut short when Alyxs snaps, "Dalia, Eryth, go get the shoes and make-up," in a harsh whisper.

A chill races down my spine at the thought of being left alone with her, and I quickly glance between Eryth and Dahlia for help.

"What, they're not here?" Dahlia replies, green leaves rustling as she searches the small space.

Behind her, Eryth's reptilian features curl into a knowing smile. "I think Alyxs needs a little time alone with the competition, Dahlia."

Competition? My brows furrow, but I keep quiet, hoping Dahlia will air her concerns.

Instead, she eyes me with a mixture of pity and dark knowing, then shrugs and says, "Right. Good luck with that." She spins on one foot and walks away, and Eryth follows, waggling all four taloned fingers of her hand in a sardonic goodbye before disappearing in the shadows.

My heartrate triples and the base of my spine begins to vibrate silent signals of approaching danger. The sensation only makes VJ throb harder, yowling for Alyxs' tentacles to complete the orgasm denied to us only minutes before.

What the fuck is wrong with you, I scream at her, revulsion crawling over my skin. *I swear, you get killed once in an objectively hot way, and then it's all your body craves. But here's the thing: Non-consensual violence is not hot, and this bitch seriously scares me. Get it together, body. Fuck!*

My skin leaps as something rubbery falls over my shoulders, but the heavy corpuscular tentacles prevent my body from following, weighing me down. I tense, muscles sending signals of conflicting escape vectors while simultaneously preparing for the incoming attack.

Seconds later, it comes in the form of a brush stroking through the tangled mess of my hair. I hiss as the tines catch on a clump of curls and jerk my head away, confusion rippling through me.

"Don't be such a baby," Alyxs chides, ripping the brush through the tangle hard enough to pull a few strands from my scalp.

My eyes water, but I squeeze my lips tight to prevent any cry from slipping out and stay perfectly still, knowing if I cry out or resist, she'll use it to justify her violence. Quiet stretches between us, and the jerky rhythm of the brush eventually smooths into a lulling rhythm.

"It's your innocence he craves, you know." Her voice carries a hard edge to it, a mixture of rage and something else I can't pinpoint.

I scoff. "I'm not a virgin," I inform her, tipping up my chin.

She snorts and moves around me, brush in hand and eyebrow raised. I half-expect her to start paddling me with it – which only amplifies the confusingly aroused throbbing between my thighs – but instead, she puts it down on a nearby counter. "Don't confuse virginity with experience. You had just enough sex to avoid the clinginess that comes with someone's first time, but not enough to be spoiled by those experiences just yet. It's why he wants you."

Biting my lip, I consider her words. She's not wrong; I'd probably had five or six sexual partners, but Jason had been my only long-term one and the only I'd tried experimenting with. "So what," I finally ask, unable to figure out what this had to do with anything. "If that was his requirement for a partner, what should it matter? Hermes told me his."

"I don't give a fuck what Hermes told you, and you'd do well not to mention that flying golden retriever in front of my lord, or he will make you regret it."

Ice crackles down my spine at the certainty in her voice. "Okay, one – that's narcissistic of him, which is pretty concerning. Two... that doesn't even begin to explain what his being into my sexual inexperience means, or why you're even telling me this, considering what a bitch you've been all night."

She snarls and is in front of me before I can blink, tentacles wrapping around my upper arms and hoisting me up with bruising force. "You know nothing!" she hisses, shaking me back and forth like I'm a rag doll. "He only ever has three of us at a time, and I'm the oldest! If you stay, he'll discard me like a hermit crab discards its shell! I can't let you – "

I'm only half-listening, my head snapping back and forth at breakneck speeds, so fast that my body just reacts, meeting her sudden violence with my own. I bring up one foot and slam it down on her face as hard as I can. It's not a good hit – the skirt they put me in is tight and I'm not high enough above her to have a good angle or leverage – but the discomforting experience of part of my foot getting lodged in her mouth is enough to get both of us to stop.

For several seconds, we just stare at each other, eyes passing through the twilight of surprise, dawning with understanding, then brightening with revulsion.

"Ugh, gross!" she sputters, pulling me away to start spitting and scrubbing at her mouth. She drops me flat on my ass, but I'm too fixated on wiping away the wetness clinging to my two littlest toes, trying to scrub away the memory of her soft mouth. For several seconds, the alcove is filled with the sounds of our shared disgust.

Gradually, revulsion fades, and I become aware of her silence, to the point where the hair on the back of my neck vibrates in alarm. I look up and catch her doubled over and glaring at me as if I was the cause of all her problems.

I roll my eyes. "Get off my fucking back, Alyxs," I bite out, scrambling to my feet. "You had no right to lay your hands on me, so it's your fault that..." I waggle my fingers toward her mouth, unable to say it, and finish, "...even happened!" Raking my hand through my still wet hair, I stare at her, utterly bewildered by her visceral. "I mean, what is your fucking problem? Why are you so threatened by me? I'm here to fuck Bacchus, sure, but you already share him, A, and B, I'm only here temporarily! I'll be moving on to the next god as soon as..."

I trail off as Alyxs face cracks wide open, like a ceramic doll smashing in slow motion in front of me. She twists away, buries her face in her hands, and begins sobbing, shoulders shaking up and down. I stare for a long moment, utterly bewildered, then narrow my eyes, suspicion blossoming. "It is temporary, isn't it, Alyxs?"

She sniffles wetly, and nods. Pauses. Shakes her head. Shrugs. "It doesn't have to be," she replies finally, voice thick with mucus and tears. "It's true, his grace is supposed to send you home after your time, but this club is a magical realm that promises freedom of choice. He'll invite you to stay. Promise to complete your journey of exploration here, which he will honor."

Black, watery tears meet mine as she twists around, and my heart breaks at the raw look of agony maligning her beauty. "And you won't be able to resist. And I will – I'll... I'll just become another fixture in his club, another has-been vying to hold his attention, even though we know we never will."

"Oh god," I exhale, horrified by what I'm hearing. "That's disgusting!" I shake my head in outright denial.

104

"I… Alyxs!" I fumble for the words, then realize what I need to say in perfect clarity. "I'll leave. Right now! Now that I know what Bacchus wants, I can just – "

Her eyes widen in alarm, and she glides across the space between us with a fluid pull of her tentacles. Her hand covers my mouth before I can even react to her moving. "You can't!" she pleads, head shaking back and forth. "Eryth and Dahlia know we were alone together and will tell him. He'll know I said something! Please!" She grabs my hands as her tentacles spread wide, dropping her to a position below me. A begging posture.

I open my mouth to reply, then pause, uncertain of what to say. On one hand, I should reject Bacchus on principle alone; using beings like they were disposable is a disgusting practice. On the other… I have no intention of staying with Bacchus. If anything, I'm about to use him like he's about to use me. I could continue as planned, do something I've always been too chickenshit to try, then politely decline his offer when he brought it up.

"Alyxs," I start. "You don't have to – "

"One minute ladies," Bacchus' voice whispers from the velvet darkness. "Why isn't she ready yet?"

Alyxs releases my hands like they are on fire and bolts back to the counter, tentacles coming up to wipe away her tears. I look around, trying to pinpoint his location only to find Eryth and Dahlia emerging into the light wearing twin malicious grins.

"Told you it'd be good," Eryth snickers, eyeing

105

Alyxs' wilted form with a gleeful zeal.

"Did you see how she threw herself at the human's feet," Dahlia retorts, more shocked than malicious. "I've never seen her so desperate! I'm so embarrassed for her."

I blink like I'm the one they verbally slapped, and look over at Alyxs, empathy growing in leaps in bounds. Not just for her, but for all three of them. I couldn't understand the strange hold Bacchus had over them, but I've seen enough to know he pitted them against each other in a way that both distracted from the inevitable truth: That Bacchus would replace them all eventually.

I open my mouth to tell them they all deserved better, but Eryth puts a scaly finger to my lips and purrs out a soft, "Shhhhhhh, little sister. We only have a few more seconds to get you ready, so no talking."

I roll my eyes but comply, letting her quickly paint my face while Dahlia helps me step into a pair of black velvet pumps. Alyxs returns a few seconds later, tears dry and a mask so thin that it only accentuates the hollow fear in her eyes. I try to catch her gaze – to convey my intentions non-verbally – but she avoids looking at me altogether and disappears behind me. I feel her fingers sliding into my hair, gathering it up at my crown, and securing it with a band.

Eryth moves aside, and suddenly I'm thrust forward into the darkness. I teeter awkwardly on the heels for several feet, completely blind to everything but the Maenads' hands on my body, guiding me.

A hand on my chest stops me. Something rolls up behind me and presses to the back of my knees hard enough that I'm forced to bend them. My ass hits something flat and soft – a chair – then it's moving, rolling forward with a throaty rattle over the stage floor.

I come to a sudden stop a few heartbeats later, and something flat and thin pushes against my plush belly. I reach out and find a hard smooth surface as far as I can touch.

"Have fun," Eryth growls in my ear. I jerk away, the hot burst of her breath on my neck making my skin crawl, then flinch at the heavy steps of their retreat. I barely have a second to wonder what I'm supposed to do when the stage lights come up, and three directed entirely at me.

Chapter Ten

Squinting against the blinding white light, I lift an arm and peer about, trying to find Bacchus or Lucifer. Or – barring that – some sort of idea of what this Temptress Punished play I'm co-starring in, since I haven't seen a script.

I quickly find a large white desk in front of me – complete with a monitor, calendar, and an expensive-looking nameplate reading: *Delilah Hansen, CEO.* I make a face at that – not the type to want to oversee anybody – and a burst of cacophonous laughter erupts around me. My muscles leap under my skin, and I look around, trying to find the audience. Four walls stand in every direction I look, completely opaque.

This is just like the shower, I realize. *The audience is probably on the other side watching me, but I can't see them.*

I bite my lip, trying to decide how to feel about it, but I'm too preoccupied with deciphering what to expect, questioning if I should call the whole thing off in light of Alyxs' revelation, growing all too aware of the lack of panties covering my ass, and how high my skirt is hiking up my thighs.

Lifting my hips, I grab the edges and try to shimmy it down without drawing too much attention to myself, but the audience hoots and hollers anyways as they realize my predicament. My cheeks heat. I look down at the white blouse unbuttoned ridiculously low, the amount of cleavage being displayed almost as ostentatious as the undersized bra forcing them together.

Is this seriously the best Bacchus can do? I think, shaking my head. *Some office scene where some hotshot underling gets to bend his boss over her desk in some gross-ass powerplay?* VJ sends delicious waves through my core at the tantalizing possibilities of such an exchange, anticipating him keeping my heels together and barely doing more than unzipping and unbuckling his pants before sliding into my slick slit…

A shudder runs through my spine, pushing the breath out of my lungs. The fantasy consumes my senses with such heat and desire that I close my eyes against it. *Stop it,* I think at my libido, clenching a fist and warring between embarrassment and hatred. *We should not find that hot, not after what we've learned! He's a jerk who uses people as objects! He's the jerk who's going to use us as objects!*

Oh, I am, am I?

My head snaps up as Bacchus' intrusive voice echoes through my mind, and looks at the door before it clicks and swings open, revealing the god of wine. The audience *oohs* and cheers like a popular character's entrance from old sitcoms, but all I can do is stare.

His outfit is different, but not in the way I anticipated. Instead of a suit, he wears a light-gray pencil skirt and white blouse with several buttons undone revealing a light dusting of his springy chest hair. The make-up is mostly unchanged, but the lipstick has gone from a glossy pink to a dark red, drawing all attention to his mouth, and his long curly hair is piled on top of his head in a messy bun. The boots are gone, replaced with a pair of black stilettos that accentuates the muscles in his fuzzy calves.

Bacchus waits for the cheers to die down, then announces, "I've got the quarterly reports from accounting," in a frazzled voice, lifting a sheaf of papers with one hand. I swallow as I realize both his hands are secured to a spreader bar running over his shoulders by a pair of manacles. "Also, Bruce from legal wants to know if we can push the meeting to four, Jane is requesting another four hundred thousand to hire two more lab techs and a full-time biologist, and your mother called to cancel dinner. Apparently, your father's got a cold."

My father's dead, I think automatically. I shake off the familiar swell of pain associated with the thought and put it aside. Clearly, these are the lines for Bacchus' play, and while I don't know how he wants me to respond, I do have something to say.

"The way you treat your Maenads is fucking disgusting," I declare. Or, at least, I try to. My mouth moves, but the words that come out aren't my own. "Thank you Bacchani. You may put those in my inbox."

"Of course," he – she? – they reply, eyelashes sweeping down demurely. However, in my head I hear, *I can't have you ruining my script, but we can talk like this. And I still prefer 'he.'* He meets my gaze with a coy little smile as he gracefully bends his knees enough so he can drop the folder in the inbox.

I could give two shits about your script, I fume. *Alyxs is terrified you're going to replace her with me. How can you let her believe that?*

Bacchani backs away with hooded lids. *Because it's true,* he replies. The indifference in his voice makes me want to scream.

What? That's crazy! She adores you! Worships the ground you walk on, and you would just... toss her aside? Like she's garbage?

"Did you need anything else, ma'am," Bacchani asks, while in my head says, *All my Maenads know the deal before they agree to take on such a role. I don't hide who I am or what will eventually happen. I can't help that I'm eternal or that existence is endless. I'm a being that will always crave new things.*

"Yes. Please tell..." Some boring set of instructions follows, delivered in an alien voice that is vaguely like mine, but I'm too shocked by his admission to pay attention.

Wait, Alyxs knew that you'd eventually ask her to leave, and still agreed? The revelation shifts my perception of the situation.

Bacchani meets my gaze, a small smirk playing on his lips. *I guess the poor dear isn't handling it as well as she thought she would. I'll be sad to see her go, but to everything, there is a season. Besides... think of all the fun we could have together.*

His eyes find mine, and the wild green of his eyes holds me captivated for several seconds, making the space tumble on all three axes. Shadows swoop in from the edges until only a trail of light connects the two of us. The weight of his desire falls upon me in a torrential waterfall, making me wet and breathless.

My body throbs under the intensity, and I almost come on the spot, images of us locked together, moving as one while a background of differently shaped individuals play behind us. It's a promise of infinite pleasure, one shaped however I want it, whenever I want it.

Stop it, I order, unnerved by how quickly my body wants to relent. *There's no way I'm going to stay here with you. You disgust me!*

The room snaps back in place, lights returning, but his smirk never wavers. *Liar,* he teases. *I can smell your desire from here.*

I roll my eyes. *Yeah, well, my body often wants things that are bad for me. Doesn't mean I let it have them.*

Ah, but indulgence is good for the soul. He

pauses, glancing off in a direction, then returns his focus to me. *The audience is getting a bit restless. Would you mind standing in front of the desk? Just to add a little action to the lines.*

Arching an eyebrow, I lean back in the chair, mouth moving and speaking lines I hadn't known existed even a second beforehand. *What, not going to puppet my body like you've commandeered my mouth?*

I just needed to borrow your delectable mouth to fill time while we hammer this out; your body remains completely under your control.

That's something, I suppose. I mean the thought privately, but I can tell by the way Bacchus' eyes gleam he hears me anyway. After a moment of consideration, I slowly stand up, figuring fulfilling his request is harmless in the grand scheme of things.

The crowd hoots and hollers, and I suddenly recall the skirt issue. Taking a few seconds, I work the scrunched-up fabric further down my thighs. My private bits are covered – I hope – and I manage to drag the edges down an inch or two before the fat of my thighs stops it. I give up a few seconds later and take a tentative step forward.

"There are a few things I need you to deliver," the script announces using my voice. I hold up a hand now gripping several folders I hadn't been a second ago.

I sigh, wondering if object impermanence is going to become an issue for me in the future, then teeter around to the front of the desk, feeling very much like a South Park character. Instructions fall from my lips, but I tune them out, considering the discussion with Bacchus thus far, and trying to decide how to proceed. In truth, I came out here with one idea, but the more I talk to the god of wine, the more confused I become.

On one hand, if Alyxs went into the situation knowing he would eventually replace her, then she didn't really have anyone but herself to blame for catching feelings, right? On the other… I have no idea if Bacchus is lying, or even using his god powers to influence her. Not to mention, treating women – or anyone, really – as disposable is despicable, and certainly demonstrates why humanity had been so willing to turn their back on him.

Yes, Bacchus interjects, face going slack with desperate hunger. *YES! That is what you can give me that Alyxs and the others can't – that need to exact justice. Find balance through retribution! I'm guilty of so many terrible things, Delilah, too many to possibly even begin to list, and I need to be punished so badly.*

"Of course," he says aloud, stalking over slowly, and – with knees together – dropping down to pluck the file out of my numb fingers. I'm acutely aware of how close his face is to my needy, aching pussy, the heat of his breath practically pushing my thighs open. My heartrate skyrockets and begins to melt as he looks up at me, green eyes molten. It's all I can do to keep from wrapping both legs around his head and riding his face to oblivion.

Do it, he pleads in the back of my brain. Aloud, he says, "Is there anything else you need, Ms. Hansen?" in a low, rumbly voice that somehow vibrates directly inside my pussy. *Punish me.*

My hands and legs tremble, and I can hear the audience holding its breath, waiting to learn what my verdict will be. So much of me wants to deny him outright – just walk out and move on to the next god on the roster.

But something else – a deeper, darker part of myself I didn't know existed – wants to embrace his suggestion and tear into him. To humiliate him by making him crawl on the floor before me, begging for forgiveness. To paddle his godly ass until it's black and blue and he couldn't even dream of sitting for weeks, forcing him to sleep face first in my pussy, which he would spend every moment licking clean of Lucifer's cum.

VJ swells and screams, at dangerous risk of imploding without any more stimuli, and I press my lips together, suppressing the moan of longing.

This isn't like me at all. All my life, I've never wanted to be dominant. I've always wanted someone else to take control.

But something has changed. A monumental shift in my core operating system. I rack my brain for what it could be, then remember Hermes' words from the bathroom. *You've unburdened yourself of a deep and significant pain, but something must fill the void where the pain was. Is this it?*

"I don't know," I hedge, and for the first time, my internal thought matches my verbal cue. Blinking, I look down at Bacchus in question.

This next bit is all you, he announces in my head, a wicked smile spreading open like curtains on a stage.

I hesitate, uncertainty rippling through me. I barely know anything about being dominant, which means I have little understanding of the rules. *What if I got carried away, or wound up hurting him?*

Good, VJ thinks, savagely turned on by the thought of a powerful being like him begging someone as weak as myself for mercy. The intensity in which she wants this is beyond anything I've ever felt before. The intensity in which I want this is beyond anything I've ever felt before.

Biting my lip, I consider him for a long moment, letting the silence between us grow. *What would I have to do?*

His Cheshire grin grows even wider. *Just say, 'Have you been a good boy, Bacchani?'*

I roll my eyes. *Okay, but for the record, your script is awful.*

Then I'll let you write the next one. Now, will you hurry up already? I – and my audience – are practically oxygen-deprived in anticipation of what you'll choose.

Taking a deep breath in and out, I steel myself and say, "Have you been a good boy today, Bacchani?"

The audience hoots and cheers, while Bacchani bats his eyelashes coquettishly. "Why of course, Ms. Hansen," he replies, as smooth as room-temperature butter. "I've been the best of boys."

The manacles pop open, the spreader clanging

to the floor. I barely hear it, too focused on his strong nose making a beeline for my pussy. My hips twitch forward, eager to meet him halfway.

"Don't believe him, Ms. Hansen," a strong voice rings out from the direction of the door.

My head jerks up toward the sound, and I freeze to see Lucifer standing there in a black pencil skirt and black silk blouse that accentuates the crimson of his skin. He too wears make-up – gold and black – and has a pair of gold stilettos strapped to his cloven hooves so high that it makes my shins cramp out of sympathy. "Meghan in accounting said he kept presenting himself to her like a cat in heat, and Jimmy from the mailroom got two blowjobs from him before lunch."

I raise an eyebrow at Lucifer's announcement, then look back at Bacchani. "Is that so?" In my mind, I ask, *Who are you in our little drama?*

Bacchani's mouth rounds around an 'o' of surprise, but I can see a mischievous gleam in his eye that belies the truth.

Lucifer replies, *I'm your other assistant, Luci.*

Slowly – and against all VJ's urgings – I back away from his mouth until I hit the desk, unexpectedly intrigued by the scene to see how it unfolds. "Well, well," I say, knowing I need to fill the silence with something, but not at all sure how to improvise a domme CEO.

Inspiration strikes a moment later with something bolder than I've ever said before, and I go with it, eager to see if this is something I could really grow into. "I'm pretty sure acting like a filthy little fuck boy isn't being a good boy," I declare, putting the point of my heel up against his shoulder and pushing him back a few inches.

My stomach churns, nervous that I've pushed things too far, but under my skin, electricity fires through nerve endings in excited lines down my limbs and spine.

You're doing perfectly, Bacchani reassures. His eyes roll back into his head, his hands wrapping around my shin and squeezing. I moan at the strength and heat there, already imagining them shoving my thighs apart and using his mouth to kiss, lick, and suck everything in between.

The sound of a wet *smack!* jerks my eyelids open, and I yank my leg away at the same time Bacchani cries out in pain, withdrawing his arm and cradling it to his chest. Looking to my left, I find Luci standing practically between us with a still-vibrating paddle the length and width of my forearm in one hand.

You're the domme this time, Delilah, he reminds me, yellow orbs giving me a pointed look. Out loud, "Bad boys don't get to touch the mistress, Bacchani. Only good boys get to do that. Bad boys get chained up and punished. Isn't that right, ma'am?"

My heart pounds as I suddenly catch onto the game, and the savage smile that forms on my lips is alien but comes with a rush of power so intoxicating that I feel like I'm floating. "Yes, it is, Luci," I exhale, knees quaking and heart pounding.

"And are you a good boy, Bacchani?" Luci asks, hooking the paddle under the other god's chin and forcing him to look up and meet my gaze.

"No," he croaks. VJ and I both dissolve at the raw honesty, guilt, fear, and need warring in the forest deity's eyes. He knows he's bad and needs to be punished for it.

And gods help me, I want to hurt him. I crave it in a way I don't understand. Even though he's never done anything to hurt me personally, I want vengeance against him. Not just for Alyxs either, but for anyone he's ever used and forsaken in his vain and selfish desire for his own pleasure.

Knowing it's what he wants only makes it hotter.

"Should I prepare him for your justice, ma'am?"

I can tell by the way Luci asks the question that it's being repeated and yank myself from the dark thoughts clouding my head. Looking around, I spot a familiar-looking goblet sitting next to my hand and scoop it up, needing a little liquid lubrication to ease VJ's urgent demands. For a long moment, I stare at the shadowy depths of the cup as if it could somehow make the decision.

Then I realize it's only me and what I want. Not Alyxs. Not Bacchus. Not Lucifer. Not Hermes.

Only me.

And what I want.

"Yes, you absolutely fucking should," I decide, the cold rage bubbling in my stomach finally boiling over, making my voice lethal.

The room erupts into thunderous applause while I take a slow sip of the sweet yet fiery liquid, savoring the burn as it slowly trickles down my center. The second mouthful I savor in my mouth before swallowing it whole. It erupts in my stomach with all the heat of an atomic bomb, yet somehow, my anger is hotter.

For once, I intend to use it.

As soon as the audience begins to quiet down, I speak. "Oh, and Luci?"

"Yes, ma'am?"

"Bring me the cane."

I have no idea if there is a cane, but it doesn't matter – my words are like the dam walls releasing as the crowd goes wild on the other side of the walls. I hear it, but I also hear both gods' thoughts in my head at the same time, their nonverbal surprise mirrored by the twin astonished expressions.

Holy shit, Luci exclaims, blinking at me.

Fuck me. Bacchani lifts his chin a second later, a triumphant grin making the apples of his cheeks practically glow. *I knew she'd come around. Just a little push and –*

Excuse me, but are we doing this? I interject coldly, unamused. *Because if we are really going to do this, then I'm the domme and my orders are to be obeyed.*

121

That is if one of you really is the good boy he assures me he is, of course. I raise the cup at Luci in salute, then drain it completely.

My dick is so hard right now, Luci exclaims, goat legs shifting back and forth inside his tight skirt.

Mine too, Bacchus echoes.

I arch an eyebrow and cross my arms. "Good boys are good listeners, Luci," I snap, and the audience behind me *oohs* in excitement, amping me on. "Unless you think I need to work two sessions today?"

"No ma'am," Luci says, shaking his head hard enough to remove the look of stunned awe from his face and only half succeeding. "I'm a very good boy, I swear."

The excitement in his voice is touched with fear, and the scintillating sound worms its way into my ear and down my spine in a wash of power that makes me tingle. My breath catches and mouth parts, and the way their eyes drop to my lips in rapt attention is enough that I could reach between my legs right now and come.

I hold it back, my anger and desire to see this through enough to keep VJ at bay.

For now, anyway.

"Then show me, and get to work," I command, and Luci snaps to and digs his fingers into the messy bun on Bacchani's head.

I watch as he drags Bacchani across the stage to the sound of the crowd's cheers, hand over my chest, fingers running absent-mindedly over my collar bones, contemplating the unfolding scene. I've never felt further from myself, yet at this moment, I'm strangely calm. I may not know what's about to unfold – or how I'm going to orchestrate it – but I'm not worried at all. If anything, I'm eager.

I stand up, about to move over and join them, when a hand on my arm pulls me short. I glance over to find Alyxs standing next to me, a metallic pitcher embossed with grapes and vines in one hand. She starts pouring before I can even express interest in a refill.

"Thanks," she whispers, spine stiff and eyes down. I know the expression of gratitude has cost her everything.

I try to think of something to say back, but she's gone before I can, disappearing through the wall in a tangle of tentacles.

Staring at the spot, I take another sip of the wine and let the warmth flow through me, heating me up. I'm acutely aware of the lights, the audience watching, and the sound of Bacchani's little gasps and cries of pain, all of them heightening my arousal to peaks and heights I'd never accomplished with anyone, including myself.

Then I turn and cross the stage, ready to indulge in an unknown fantasy where I'm in complete control.

God, I am so ready for this, VJ breathes. For once, we're in total agreement.

Chapter Eleven

*I*n the time it takes for me to process my decision and get more wine from Alyxs, Luci has bound Bacchani's arms behind his back, one folded on top of the other and secured with an elaborate series of knots. I've seen enough porn to recognize Shibari – a Japanese bondage technique.

My heart skips a beat then lands in a low jog. *This is happening. I'm really in control.* I take a small sip from my cup and pluck at the edges of my blouse, trying to cool the rush of heat racing across my skin, then step forward, reentering the light and the scene.

We're in the section of the office set up with low couches around a coffee table. The table is gone now – Bacchani takes its place – but the seating remains. I lean against the side of a couch and cross my arms, watching.

Luci finishes securing the rope to a metal loop on the wall, then shoves Bacchani down onto his knees, pulling the rope tight around his upper and forearms. The god of wine throws his head back and cries out, Adam's apple bobbing up and down.

I can't stop the dark impulse from hi-jacking control. Pushing off the couch, I cross the stage between us and grab his hair, holding his head back and exposing his throat to me. His cry becomes a ragged gasp, and I lean in and rub my face against his, letting the rough facial hair scrape over my cheeks and chin, marking my scent on him.

What am I doing? I freeze, surprised at not only the urge but at how I acted upon it without any consideration. Once again, I'm struck by how alien I feel, like some dark entity has slipped into a thin layer just between my intentions and my execution.

Don't overthink this, Delilah, I think, shaking it off. *You've just had a lot of booze, and you are living for this fantasy made real. It's okay to get into it.*

Absolutely, concurs Luci, golden orbs meeting mine and black lips splitting wide to reveal fanged teeth.

I let go of Bacchani's head and step back, glaring at Luci for the unwelcome intrusion. *No more listening in on my thoughts, either of you,* I command. *They're private from here on out.*

Ugh, fine! Bacchani scoffs, eyelashes fluttering. *Just pull my hair and do that thing with the neck again! That was hot.*

I narrow my eyes at him. Clearly, he's still enjoying this, which means we aren't doing enough. "He needs a noose, too. One that matches the slack his arms have."

Luci's eyes widen, browless lids furrowing, then smiles in delight. The interest in his eyes intensifies, and he nods. "Yes, ma'am."

Snapping his fingers, a thick brown rope appears in a puff of black smoke, the slip-knotted end in one hand, the coiled length in the other. He quickly affixes it around Bacchani's neck, then secures it to a secondary hook a bit higher up. There is some slack in the rope, but not much, so depending on how far Bacchani leans forward...

My imagination takes over with images of his face turning blue and eyes bulging while his tongue stretches mere millimeters away from my clit. Choking himself, just on the off chance he can pleasure me.

VJ pulses, sending involuntary muscle spasms so intense that my hips wriggle back and forth in a desperate bid for friction.

God, I want to get off! I'd do anything just to –

I don't have to do anything, I realize in a flash of inspiration that is the rolling thunder before a building storm. A wicked smile forms on my lips.

"Luci, come here," I say, crooking my index finger at him. I hate when people do it in real life, but here, I know it will only add to the illusion for them and make it a bit more fun for me.

"But... I have to put on his cock cage, mistress," Luci pouts petulantly.

His cock cage? My grin grows by leaps and bounds, and I look down at Bacchani with an unexpected surge of pleasure and surprise. *You're really going for this, aren't you? You really want to be punished.*

Even though the minx isn't supposed to be listening, he lifts his gaze up from the edge of my skirt to my eyes, and projects, *Fuck yes, I do. I need it. I'm awful, Delilah. Horrible and monstrous. Whatever you feel I deserve as justice will never be enough.*

The raw sincerity in his eyes is all the permission I need, and the words not only help; they inspire. "Never mind that – I need my good boy over here to take off these constricting clothes and relieve some of the tension this little man-slut's bad behavior has created. Have Alyxs take over for you."

The audience's collective gasp sucks the air out of the room, and for several agonizing heartbeats, no one moves or says anything. Bacchani and I stare the other down; his eyes gleaming in sullen anger, mine in righteous satisfaction.

"You said you wanted justice," I murmur, pitching my voice low enough so only he and Luci can hear. "This is a step toward it."

He looks down a few seconds later and gives a tight nod of his head, surrender bleeding into his shoulders and spine.

"Luci, text Alyxs and – "

"Already done, mistress," the devil interrupts, phone appearing and thumbs moving in a blur. The chirp of a message being sent sounds a heartbeat later, then he's tossing his phone over his shoulder. "After all, I am your very very good boy, right?" he purrs sultrily, and the audience laughs. He doesn't wait for my response, simply shoots Bacchani a smug look before clomping over to me, hooves in heels thumping heavily on the wooden stage.

My heart skips a beat as he steps into me and undoes my blouse, button by button. I take a sip of my wine and hold my breath, trying not to break the spell weaving between us.

Gently, he eases one breast out from its compressing elastic cage and gently lays it over the fabric and underwire. Even though the band is still tight underneath, I can't help the sigh of relief I feel at the weight of it slipping free. All is silent as he repeats the process with the other, then stares at them for several long moments, not moving.

Nipples tightening at the intense scrutiny, I breathe, "Touch me," in his ear before nibbling on the soft ridge. It's an order, but it feels like I'm begging.

He obeys nonetheless, strong hands coming up and cradling them gently. If he's offended or repulsed by their oblong shape or lack of bounce, he doesn't show it. If anything, his face is slack with awe, like I'm a goddess, and somehow, he – unworthy bastard though he is – he gets to touch. Fingers tighten and flex, massaging into the soft flesh and penetrating deep into the ache and soreness that came from the constricting garment, and I throw my head back and moan loudly.

Shit, I'm being so noisy!

My cheeks heat, and I'm immediately distracted by the hushed whispers and heavy breathing pouring in through the walls. Then it all dies down, and I realize the audience is waiting. Watching my move with bated breath.

Lust surges and hips jerk in response. I go lightheaded from the pleasure of Luci's touch, the alcohol burning through my veins and pouring into the liquid inferno now boiling over between my thighs. I can't seem to catch my breath, too focused on his fingers and how they stroke over my flesh. It's pure torture, and yet he's so tender, treating my flesh with a reverence I've never experienced before. It's like I'm a goddess being tormented through worship. Beloved while also denied.

Another groan against me as my nipples tingle in anticipation of his touch as it draws near then burns in pain when he inexplicably moves away. I arch my back, trying to rub it into his hand, but the minx deftly avoids me, sliding the tips of his talons down and over my solar plexus and abdomen before returning.

I remember I'm in charge a second later, and say, "Suck them," before wrapping my hand around the smooth base of his skull and tugging him down. This time he doesn't resist, dipping forward and pulling one hard bud into his hot, wet mouth. I throw back my head to avoid the sharp points of his horns, which only makes my breathlessness increase and stability decrease. Reaching out, I grab onto his upper arm and hold tight, determined not to collapse on the floor.

Sharp teeth scrape over a nub, sending jolts of electricity directly to my pussy.

"*Uuuuuuuuuuuunnnnnnnggggggg.*"

At first, I think the sound comes from me, somehow escaping through my rapidly dissipating control over my body. But when I can't seem to make it stop, I open my eyes and look between Lucifer's horns toward the source.

Bacchani stares at us, mouth open and eyes ravenous. He's leaning at a seventy-five-degree angle, which has brought both the noose and the ropes securing his arms taut. I hold his gaze for several seconds while Luci sucks at my teat, making VJ throb and weep until I can't bear the sweet torment anymore.

"Get this off of me," I command, pushing Luci's mouth off me and shrugging one arm out of the blouse in a desperate need to be free of all constrictions. He quickly obeys, stripping the garment off me, then reaches both arms around my waist for the bra. His face looms extraordinarily close to mine. Heat radiates off him like he's a furnace, and I start tilting my head back to get a breath of fresh air. I pause when I see his pink forked tongue poking from between his black lips while he fiddles with the hooks. It's so undeniably sweet and sexy, all I want to do is lean close and lick it.

Suddenly, I realize the Lord of Hell has been

balls deep inside me, yet I haven't gotten anything as mundane or intimate as a kiss.

Another injustice in need of correction, a voice urges, and I wholeheartedly agree.

I reach up and cup his cheek, and he jerks in surprise, golden eyes with Saturn-shaped silhouettes studying me with uncertainty. Sliding my hand around to the back of his neck, I grip it firmly and pull his head toward mine. I can feel the barely contained strength in his neck and shoulders flex against my hand, wordlessly signaling he could easily resist my pull if he wants to, but he doesn't. Instead, he leans his head down toward me and seals my mouth with his.

My lungs burn and I exhale the breath I've been holding, savoring the silky feel. I immediately pull his lower lips between mine and suck, tongue tracing lightly over the edge. He shudders and steps into me, pressing the front of his body into mine. Flesh burns where we touch, but I don't care, too lost in the curious sensation of his tongue slipping into my mouth and stroking over mine. I moan and try to wrap one leg around his hip, but the tightness of the skirt prevents me from reaching. VJ is still completely exposed, but there's nothing for her needy muscles to contract around but air.

I break off the kiss with a whimper. "The skirt!" The comment is half-whine, half-guttural, all me, and Luci squats down and begins to yank. I gasp impatiently and finish taking off the bra, freeing my tits and letting cool air wash over them.

As I do, I look over Luci's back at Bacchani, and find him even closer, the noose on his throat tighter and face a little pinker. Glancing down at his skirt reveals his thick erection caught inside the folds of his own skirt, and I realize Alyxs still isn't on stage.

"Where is she," I ask in a loud, impatient voice. "I don't like waiting."

As if I've given a secret cue, the door opens and Alyxs enters. Her toga is gone – replaced with yet another business outfit that mirrors our own - and her black eyes are now partially hidden behind a pair of horn-rim glasses.

"Apologies, Mistress," she says, ducking her head. "It took me a second to find this." She holds up her hands, which are cupping a black metallic device. It's smaller than I imagined it would be, yet comes with a series of internal nubs along the bars that promise to dig in painfully as soon as he gets aroused.

Thanks for coming, I direct at her, hoping she can hear.

I know she can with the annoyed look I receive from her a second later. *This won't work, you know. It won't be the first time I've dominated him. If anything, he's only into it because you want me here. He'll still want to be rid of me tomorrow, no matter what happens tonight.*

I hear the pain in her words and feel my anger at Bacchus growing. *I didn't bring you out here to win him back,* I inform her coolly. *I asked you out here so you can show him exactly how you're feeling.*

She blinks, onyx eyes widening, and the grin I supply is one of mostly bared teeth. *Make sure to make it burn,* I add, and the smile she gives me is so sly and filled with malicious intent that I almost worry about what I've unleashed on the wine god.

Almost.

She hurries off to get to work, and I focus back on Luci, ready to continue my own torment of Bacchani. He struggles to work the edges down over my thick thighs and knows it is a war he can never win. Frustration and need send me bouncing up and down in little hops, trying to help loosen the fabric.

As soon as I do, the fat parts of my body slap together obscenely, and I freeze, all my confidence melts into a deep humiliation in an instant. I'm painfully aware of how repulsive my loose and fluffy folds are, and close my eyes, anticipating the jeers about to be thrown at the ill-formed meat sack that is my body.

"Whoohoo!" comes a feminine cry from somewhere beyond the walls, and it's quickly followed by similar cheers and catcalls so loud, it's deafening.

I exhale shakily and open my eyes to find Luci staring up at me, the side of his face pillowed against my thigh. He squeezes my knee reassuringly and I realize he noticed me falter. Shooting him a nervous smile, I gesture down to my skirt. "Can you just get me out of this already," I ask in a low voice, self-conscious by the fact that nothing is going smoothly.

He nods, horns bobbing, then reaches out with one black claw. My breath catches in my lungs, and I go perfectly still, not willing to move an inch lest he slices me. Fabric rips, filling the space around us with an intoxicating sound, and the hair on my thighs stand on end as they're exposed to cool air. Another jerk of Luci's hand pops the band around my belly free, and finally, I'm completely bare. Naked for all to see.

My nipples harden to icy points, flesh pounding in time with my heart, but it's the screams and cries of the crowd that ratchets me higher and higher. Bacchani writhes in pain as Alyxs roughly forces the cock cage around his erect member, making it shrink down and deflate.

I tip my head to one side to inspect his cock, but I can't see anything past her hands and the black cage. Bacchani tosses his head back and forth so hard the messy bun goes lopsided, then lets out a final cry before Alyxs closes the cage with a sharp click. His chest heaves and throat work convulsively, and all I can think about is crossing over and mounting him right there.

But that would be giving him what he wants, which is the opposite of tonight's exercise.

I remember the goblet in my hand and take a swig. The flavor is barely noticeable at this point, so much of it is humming through my blood and numbing my senses. I glance down at Luci and find him waiting patiently at my feet, like a dog awaiting his mistress' command. The imagery of the demonic prince, known for his arrogance and defiance, kneeling in front of me, ready to serve, is so erotic that I clench tight against the tsunami of fluid dripping from my pussy.

Fuck! I think, trying to fight for control. I'm supposed to set the pace in the scenario, but all I can think about is the increasing pressure mounting in my mons. I want to get off so bad.

Why can't you? VJ retorts, forcing our hips forward a millimeter or two. *Bacchani's the one being punished, not you.*

She's right. I open my mouth to give the command, when he suddenly interjects, "Should we give Bacchani a demonstration, Mistress?"

"Demonstration?"

"One that shows him exactly what a good boy gets to do to his mistress."

VJ yowls, and the sound it creates in my head is nothing compared to the gurgling choking sound coming just past Luci. I glance back at Bacchani to find him now at a sixty-degree angle, face red and noose tight enough to make the surrounding skin start to bulge.

"Fuck yes," I reply to Luci, knowing it will drive Bacchani mad. "Alyxs, make sure he keeps focused completely on us, and spank him anytime he loses focus. Luci, let's start with... Bad boys don't get to touch; only good boys do."

Chapter Twelve

I don't get a chance to see Bacchani's reaction – Luci moves too fast. Wrapping a hand around my ankle, he wedges his shoulder under my thigh and dives face-first into my mound. His long tongue immediately finds the top of my slit, snaking down and over my clit and urethra before gliding against sensitive nerves around my entrance. The forked tip slips in a second later, teasing the side of my inner labia in light strokes. I gasp, legs shaking violently, and grab onto his horns to keep from falling.

Both his hands come up and over my ass cheeks, gripping them tightly. Then he's hefting me in one smooth motion, keeping my crotch tight to his face. I let out a sharp cry of surprise, completely unnerved and turned on at how easily he does it. He takes a few steps back and deposits me on my back on a couch, then continues to cradle my hips and lap up my juices.

Using his horns as leverage, I grind my pussy against his face in search of any hard edges I can use to get off, already fantastically close. Strong fingers find my nipples and pinch them tight, sending waves of pain and pleasure throughout my body that make me convulse.

Thwap! "*AAAGH*! Fuck, Alyxs! That's too hard!"

"Fuck you, Bacchani – you deserve this! I gave you decades of my life!" I twist my head and watch as Alyxs draws back a wide paddle on a long handle, then brings it down and around, smacking Bacchani squarely on his left ass cheek with a resounding slap.

He yells and jerks forward, then screams and pulls back as his caged junk flops down against his upper thighs, making the folds of dark flesh protruding through the bars smack wetly in a way that looks excruciating. He struggles and pulls against his bonds, trying to break free, but the ropes hold fast.

Is it an act, I dimly wonder. *It has to be, right? He's a god. Nothing can really hurt a god.* I think it, but I'm unconvinced. His face is red and swollen, sweat pouring from his forehead and cutting lines through his make-up.

Normally, such a display would lead to a surge of empathy, but instead, all I feel is a sense of rightness and savage satisfaction. It's as if some imbalance is being corrected. It isn't finished – not by a long shot – but it is coming.

"No," Luci growls, breaking the seal over my clit. "I get all your focus! I get all your pleasure. I'm the good boy!"

He rips his arms out from under my back and slides up my body, blocking my view of Bacchani. I inhale sharply at the intense cast on his features, but he cuts it short by sealing his mouth to mine and forcing his tongue in deep. The taste of my pussy and his tongue fills my mouth, and my eyes roll back into my head. Grabbing his shoulders, I wrap my legs around his haunches, wanting him to fill me the same way his tongue is.

Luci catches my hips with one hand and breaks the kiss, resting his heated forehead against mine. His heavy heated pants caress my face and neck. I feel him struggle for control. It's intoxicatingly hot, and I fight against his hold, needing to feel him deep inside. The hips caging my legs buck; I feel him giving in…

Then he emits a loud groan and slides down my body, muttering, "Good boys get to kiss their mistress everywhere they want," as he kisses down my cheek and neck.

"*Unnnngh!*" comes Bacchani's moan, followed by another sharp *thwap* and cry of pain. The soundtrack only adds to my growing frenzy, clit throbbing in time with my heartbeat. Luci's mouth closes around one nipple, then the other, teeth scraping and sucking hard, but the sensation barely registers through the buzzing of my genitals. I need so much more. I need to come.

"Please," I cry, and the sound is echoed by a choked cry from Bacchani. "Be the very best boy and make me come!"

Luci releases my nipple with a soft pop and suddenly he's gone, cold air flooding the space where his heated body had been. I awkwardly sit up on my elbows, afraid I've offended him or ruined the fantasy when the sound of tearing fabric cuts over the sharp thwaps. I follow it and find his skirt in tatters around his thighs, but the erect length of his spade-shaped cock jutting out past his goat-like haunches.

It's even more impressive in this light, the red scalloped edges seemingly fuller and more swollen than before. VJ clenches at the size and conical girth as it connects to the base. My mouth goes dry and vision white, the sheer agony of my desire making me mindless.

"Yes," I shout as his hands roughly pick me up. "Show Bacchani what good boys get!"

My center of gravity sways and shifts as he adjusts us both, and my vision returns as he settles me onto his lap on the couch. We're now mere inches from Bacchani's scarlet and sweaty face. My vision doubles as he leans forward, mouth open, trying to bury his face in my molten hot quim, pulling against the rope, choking himself to get to me.

I whimper and try to meet him halfway, but Luci keeps his hand tight on my hip bone, preventing me. I scream and struggle, mindless to end the torment thrumming through the lower half of my body.

The lord of darkness lifts me up and leans me forward a few inches until my tits hang just millimeters from Bacchani's hungry mouth. I arch my back, trying to feed them to him, but Luci pulls me back.

For a moment, my heart screams with a fiery rage at being denied yet again, but it is cut short by the tip of his arrow-shaped cock head spreading my entrance open, scalloped edges skipping over hypersensitized nerves. I gasp and jerk back, shoulder and head meeting his chest with a wet slap.

"Fight it," he whispers urgently, and his breath tickles the short hairs on the back of my neck and behind my ear. "Just long enough to watch his face as you break apart on me."

Panting, body quivering from strain, I open my eyes and peer through the haze of lust and booze and focus on Bacchani. His face is swollen, skin so red it's almost purple. The noose is cinched tight around his throat, the skin around it practically spilling over the edges. He's so close to the junction of my thighs that I can feel the hot ragged air of his breath puffing against the tuft of hair covering my mound.

Slowly, Luci fills me, sliding between slick walls, spreading them apart, and gliding against them. My mouth falls open, but I can't scream, the air in my lungs frozen in shock from the sheer pleasure of his penetration. Nerves denied for so long suddenly fire all at once, and my muscles slacken and retract around his delicious shape. In a heartbeat, I'm orgasming, limbs spasming wildly as ripples of pleasure.

A heavy weight wraps over my chest, another cradles my crotch, massaging the flesh, and I dimly feel Luci inside me, riding my contractions with his thick length. He somehow catches a wave, and I suddenly feel a second orgasm building on the back of the first one.

"No!" I manage, mouth dry, body clenching with panic. "Too soon!"

"Nuh-uh," he breathes in a childish tone. "Good boys get to make their mistress come. Over and over and over again."

Something buzzes unexpectedly against my clit, and I shift away trying to escape. It follows, chasing the hypersensitized nub and finding it. It gyrates intensely enough that everything below my waist clenches as waves of pain and pleasure emanate from it, and I look down. Red fingers tipped with black talons cradle a familiar egg-shaped object.

It's just like the one I have at home. The thought is lost a second later as he works his thick length in and out of me while swirling the vibrator around. It takes only a handful of seconds before I orgasm all over again.

It's less intense yet leaves me exhausted and aware of nothing but my heart, the convulsing muscles of my quim, and the connective tissue in between. The rest of me is spread out like soft butter on toast.

I drift, the familiar cocoon of endorphins coupled with the alcohol in my system creating a soft inky cloud enticing me to give myself over to it. I realize I haven't slept since my resurrection in Duat, and while the entire exchange with Bacchus and Lucifer is the most incredible sexual moment of my life, I can feel my stamina fading.

"Oh no you don't, precious," Luci's voice slices through the inviting void of unconsciousness. I moan and ignore him, wanting to drift off, but an insistent pressure from my bladder begins to assert itself.

No! Panicking, I tip my hips forward, trying to avoid the vibrator buzzing between my lips, fighting the urge my contracting muscles are building toward. Luci groans, his cock picking up speed. Looking down the length of my body, I see his black and red member sliding in and out of me like a steam engine, while Bacchani watches from millimeters away.

The god is now purple, his breath a sharp wheeze. Tears, snot, and drool stream down his face. Behind him, I hear the *thwap, thwap, thwap* of the paddle slamming into him, but his jerks are minimal, like he has nowhere to go.

I clench down on my muscles tighter, fighting the rising tide. "Wait!"

"No! Good boys don't have to wait! They get to shoot their load deep inside their mistress' creamy cunts!" He drives himself in to the hilt, then emits a wrangled cry, hips twitching in obvious signs of release. The vibrator continues to grind tight against the section of my slit still capable of feeling and my control slips.

Meeting Bacchani's eyes over the peaks and valleys of flesh and between us, I try to give warning. I barely make out the 'm' sound when the third orgasm splits me in half. Liquid sprays around the toy, splattering Luci's fingers and Bacchani's face.

I freeze, hand covering my mouth, and stare down at him, mortified to my very core. *I just ejaculated in his face! I didn't even know I could do that, and now, I just...* I gasp as VJ pulses, sending an aftershock of pleasure jolting through me and another liquid spurt, cheeks burning red-hot.

"I'm so sorry," I say, but my voice is barely audible, clenched tight. Clearing it with a small cough, I try again. "I'm so – "

"Ready to let this bad boy clean up your good boy's mess?" Luci interrupts. Gently, he withdraws his limp cock from my wet and swollen folds. The movement sends a smattering of confused signals through me, and for several moments, I'm lost to the blinding, rolling ecstasy thrumming through every muscle and leaving them soft goo in the aftermath.

My brain dissolves into a hazy state, saturated by the mixture of endorphins and alcohol. Once again, I'm drawn to sleep, carried on a warm glowing cloud. I drift, absolutely content, when a shadow cuts over the light warming me from above.

I groan and try to turn away from it, but all I can manage is my head flopping to the other side. Then something soft and wet slides over the raw edges of my entrances, and I hiss, eyes snapping open.

In front of my face is a hairy thigh, and I follow it up to the dangling cock cage. *Bacchani's straddling my head while his mouth gets to work below, following Luci's order to clean up his cum.* The realization is followed by, *Is this seriously still happening?*

144

I close my eyes and try to will it away, but the insistent licking from between my legs scrapes over raw skin, sending tiny surges of pain that pull me further and further away. I buck and tilt my hips away from him, mentally screaming, *I can't! It's too much!*

He ignores me by sealing his mouth to my pussy with an obnoxious slurping sound, tongue roughly probing in and out of my bruised entrance.Crying out, I try to escape his mouth, the agony of being touched so soon after so much overwhelming. *I've never had this many back-to-back before, and it's beginning to hurt.*

Nonsense, Bacchani replies. He slides his tongue delicately along my swollen lips, leaving a delicious shiver in his wake – a line of pleasure cutting over the agony elsewhere. Weaving up my folds, he encircles my inflamed nub without touching it, lifting me to a peak so fast that I'm teetering on the edge of climax. All my body resists, clenching tight to fight the fall. *You just need to build a little endurance.*

He punctuates his statement by dragging his stubble against my clit, creating a new sensation. I scream, body resisting the urge to let go for a fourth time. Strained muscles pull and clench wetly and a deep ache helps keep the orgasm at bay, but just barely. *When is this going to end?*

As if in answer to my question, a sound sucking catches my ears – a feat given how hard my blood is pounding behind them – and I roll my head back, making the world beyond Bacchani's legs upside down.

Luci sits with Alyxs perched on one haunch.

Mona Ventress

They're stroking and petting each other, but their focus is completely on me and Bacchani's ass. Luci's cock is already hard again, jutting forth between his thighs like a spade ready to split earth. As I watch, one of Alyxs' tentacles curls up the shaft and wraps around it, working up and down.

At the same time, three more stretch out toward me, two sliding up and over my shoulders while the other works up Bacchani's thigh. The slick, muscular appendages work over the curve of my breasts, delicate tips curling around my nipples. They curl and squeeze tight, and my back arches in response to new stimuli.

Bacchani's hips jerk forward at the same moment while Luci gives a strangled groan, and for several moments all three of us are held in thrall by the octopus woman's clever tentacles. Then Bacchani gives out a wrangled cry and plants himself face-first right between my thighs.

I cry out in pain as he viciously sucks and laps every swollen crease. My nervous system is burnt out, but he neither notices nor cares, too fixated on devouring my folds to worry about the agony it's creating. I do everything I can to signal him to stop, from kicking my legs to biting his inner thighs, but it only eggs him on.

Perhaps it's punishment for ejaculating all over his face, a voice taunts.

I reject the notion, reminding myself tiredly that this is Bacchani's punishment. That helps trigger

146

something, and as I look around, my eyes finally find the cock cage dangling only a few inches above my face. It takes a herculean effort to sit up, but when I do, I run my tongue over one of the areas where his flesh bulges through the bars, pressing into it.

"No! Ah! Fuck!" Bacchani breaks away from my cunt with a wrangled hiss, hips jerking violently. The cage clicks against my teeth, but I quickly grab on to steady it and continue to suck, my turn to be oblivious to his gurgling sounds of protest. The skin is soft and hot under my lips and mouth, with a fascinating texture and slightly salty taste.

Even as I register those details, a sickeningly sweet and pungently sour taste explodes over my taste buds, and I reflexively pull my head back, sputtering.

"What was that?" I ask, scrubbing at my mouth with the back of one hand. I want to spit it out, but it clings to the inner walls of my cheeks and creeps past them toward my throat. It hits my salivary glands and they automatically flood, washing the flavor to the back of my palate and down my throat.

A burn unlike anything I've felt before hits my esophagus a moment later, triggering a short and smelly burp, and I suddenly place the flavor. *It's a concentrated version of his wine! That's what he meant when he said they got drunk on him!*

It drives a molten line down my chest and explodes in my stomach with a rush of heat that makes all my pain melt away and my muscles go liquid. My vision swims and head goes woozy. Time slows to a

Mona Ventress

pinprick of speed, and I close my eyes, the lids too heavy to remain up.

"It was too much for her," I dimly hear Luci chide.

"Then just prop her up to watch and let's keep going."

Hands grab me and heft me up; drag me across the floor. Everything becomes a blur after that, conscious and drunken images flowing through my mind like a merry-go-round...

...watching as Luci and Alyxs tease Bacchani as they string up his arms using a pair of manacles on chains...

...taking turns spanking him while Luci and Alyxs keep me upright...

...Luci leaning over and kissing Bacchani deeply as he places the tip of his cock between those tight little butt cheeks and thrusts...

...Alyxs cuddling me from behind, keeping me awake while the men play. There is a lapse in conversation and our eyes meet. Her gaze then drops to my mouth, and my breath catches. She leans in, her soft lips pressing against mine and I can't stop the moan of want as I experience my first kiss with a woman. Her mouth is everywhere, tentacles following behind and it doesn't take me long to explode...

...looking out and realizing the walls are gone – as is most of the stage – and our small circle of light is surrounded by writhing bodies in various stages of undress, all staring at us, worshipping us...

...waking to both men licking my pussy with tender care, pushing the line of pleasure and pain that twists and morphs until I am shaking, creaming, coming, body dissolving to nothingness...

Chapter Thirteen

$\mathscr{I}$ wake up in waves, each one carrying with it the queasiness and pain that comes after a night of drinking. My head is first, coming to awareness despite the thick cobwebs slowing my receptors, a dull ache in the base of my skull and temples promising a monumental migraine. My stomach is next, the acid inside bubbling just under the surface, making my gut squirm alarmingly. A soft belch escapes me, and I grimace at the resulting stench coming from my dry and sticky mouth. Lifting my head slowly, I open my eyes a sliver to try and get a sense of my surroundings.

The room is oppressively dark, but as my bleary eyes adjust, I see small flickering orbs in sporadic places, casting dim pools of orange light. Strange lumpy shadows make up the floor below, but my hangover makes it difficult to focus.

Groaning, I sit up and press a hand to my

forehead, trying to relieve the building, and my stomach lurches. I gag and cover my mouth with a hand, fighting the roiling mass trying to break free of my gullet.

"Mmmmm, good morning, gorgeous," Bacchus' voice rumbles into my ear. Hot lips and rough facial hair press against my forehead, sending confusing shivers through my skin, and I glance over to find Bacchus, regarding me under heavy eyelids. "How did you sleep?"

"I… uh… Errrrp." An obnoxious burp forces itself from my throat before I can clap my hand over my mouth to stop it. "I'm so sorry," I breathe. "I think I might be – "

"Shhhh," he interrupts, pulling me tight against his chest. "You don't want to disturb the group, do you?"

I look around, confused, then realize the lumpy objects on the floor are bodies, all in various states of undress, the sounds of their even breathing and snores filling the room. We're still in the club, but on a large circular bed in the middle of the room, surrounded by sleeping creatures.

"Thanks to your performance last night, we had one of the most successful shows in a long time."

My cheeks flush at the pride in his voice, but truthfully, everything after the desk is a blur. "Oh, um… you're welcome," I manage, unable to come up with anything better. The mass writhing in my belly swells up, and I close my eyes and take a deep breath, trying to force it down, but I know it's only a matter of time.

"Where's Luci?" I ask, trying to distract myself.

"Oh, he had to leave," Bacchus replies. "But he was very impressed by you. He even left you his card, which I took the liberty of sending to your home. Although I doubt you'll be needing it."

I squint at him with one eye, only able to catch half his words through my swollen brain. "Huh?"

His hands encircle my upper arms and he pulls me into his lap, sliding his legs in between mine and spreading them wide. I moan as VJ awakens with a vengeance, somehow ready to slide down his pole like an on-call firefighter with a blaze to battle. "You were incredible last night," he breathes, hands coming up to stroke my arms. "How you handled yourself – the things you did!? Simply sensational."

Velvet lips skim my shoulder, sending shivers down my spine even as a cold sweat erupts at my hairline. My body fights a war between lust and hangover and loses viciously. I need to find a bathroom, drink some water, and sleep. "Uh… okay? Where's the – "

"Stay with me," he interrupts, finger sliding over my lip to shush me. "Release my cock from the cage and accept me deep inside."

"What?" I groan, shifting in his hold. My brain sloshes around in my head, making my stomach curdle, but his comment creates enough confusion that I can ignore it for a bit longer. "No one let you go last night? Oh my god!"

I look down between my legs, and sure enough, his dick is still inside the cage. The skin is protruding less – probably because he isn't fighting an erection – but as I watch, it starts to puff up again. Immediately, I spot the latch and reach for it.

"Yes, baby girl," he hisses, tossing his dark curls over one shoulder. "Set me free. Let me fill you with my essence until all you can feel is me in your blood."

My fingers stroke over the latch before his words can register and it slips free, the two pieces of the cage clattering on the ground.

I gasp as his dick inflates to a considerable size, eyeing the strange and unique shape with a mixture of apprehension and lust. From above, it looks like a normal, uncircumcised cock – a bit dark in shade, and thrusting up from a thick tangle of dark pubic hair at the base. But underneath… The flesh is stretched and elongated into rippling furls with thin, swirling ridges. The shape, size, and placement remind me of wood ear mushrooms climbing up the side of a tree. As I stare, the furls plump and a few golden drops of liquid droplets bead up from between the folds.

"What is that?"

Running his forefinger along the furls, he collects a small bead on the tip and holds it up to me. "You had a taste last night, don't you remember? When you were tormenting my cock with that sweet, sadistic mouth of yours." His eyes roll to the back of his head as a shudder races through him. "Don't you remember how delicious it was?"

He holds it out to me, and I stare, cheeks salivating, even as my stomach churns. "I'm not sure." My speech is slow, mouth dry. Even as I try to resist, it calls, the haze and pleasure of last night like a siren's song.

Smirking knowingly, he holds his finger closer to my lips, golden droplet clinging tight to the curved tip. "It's okay if you put it in your mouth once or twice," he promises, voice and eyes dark. Magnetic.

I stick out my tongue as he brings it close, then pulls it away last minute to lick it up. I stare at him, confused, then give a sharp, "Ah," of pain when he grabs my hips and thrusts against me, soft furls sliding over the raw and swollen edges of my pussy. My tummy reasserts itself, the memory of the taste in my mouth and the alcohol it contained makes me want to heave. I push the swollen mass a few inches down my esophagus, but I can tell by its buoyancy that it's a losing battle.

"Your cunt and your ass, however," he continues, oblivious of my state, "are completely different." Between my legs, my genitals warm, then glow, and I feel a rush of alcohol surge up my neck and into my head, making it go woozy.

My stomach revolts immediately, still too raw from last night's debauchery, and I fight the pressure growing at the top of my belly. "After a while, you'll be more tolerant, and I'll forever be a part of your bloodstream – something you'll depend on for your entire life. I'll give you everything you want. Anything you desire. But you need to understand that if I do, you'll be abandoning the deal you made with other gods. You'll be mine and mine alone."

Sweat beads on the back of my neck and forehead, trying to chill my burning flesh. "What are you saying?" I manage thickly, focusing on my breathing to keep from vomiting.

"Just as I said," Bacchus replies, voice matter of fact. "My agreement with the others is that I won't get you addicted to my essence. A taste is fine." He cups my jaw, thumb dragging over my lower lip. He seems not to notice the beads of sweat that have accumulated there in the wake of my growing distress. "But a direct injection, so to speak, would mean my essence would be absorbed directly into your bloodstream, and you'd never want to be rid of me. I'd be inside you always, pleasing you, making you want to do whatever makes me happy. You'd protect me. Hold me. Put on little plays to please me. Fuck whoever and whatever I want, whenever I want it."

His words weave a dark tapestry of debauchery and hedonism. It's a powerful lure, or would be if I wasn't so nauseated. "What about the other gods," I ask, remembering Anubis' concerns they would come for me. "Won't they fight you?"

"Those pathetic has-beens are powerless compared to me. All I need do is seal my realm from them, and you'll be safe from them for the rest of your life." His hands drag down my sides. "Doesn't that sound great?"

I close my eyes and sway back and forth. In truth, nothing sounds good. All I can think about is my stomach, and how much it hates me. "I'm not sure," I finally reply. "I need to think."

Bacchus scoffs. "Think? About what? You'd be at the center of the biggest, most epic party in a thousand lifetimes. We'll get high and fuck whenever and however we want. I know you want so much more than you've tasted thus far, which is why you'd make the perfect Maenad. Stay with me, Delilah."

Even knowing he intended to ask it the night before, I'm still surprised when he does. I'm certain I made my decision clear last night. Even still, there's a naked want in his voice, and for a moment, I wonder if – beyond all reason – the ancient god has fallen head-over-heels in love with me.

Then my stomach turns and the pain in my brain intensifies, cutting through the bullshit. *He just said, 'You'd protect me. Hold me. Put on little plays to please me. Fuck whoever and whatever I wanted, whenever I wanted it.' That's so one-sided. What about my needs? What about what I want? This isn't about me – it's just about him – just like every other man.*

I immediately think of Hermes and his differences, and for a moment, everything ailing me goes calm and still. Looking around at the crowd of bodies around us, I search for the familiar gold mop of curls in the mass of bodies. *He said he'd be watching – does that mean he stuck around for the orgy? Is he here somewhere?*

157

"What is it," Bacchus asks, following my gaze. "What are you looking for?"

"Hermes," I reply automatically. "I want to leave."

Bacchus throws me off his lap so fast that I land in a sprawl at his feet. "My brother?!" he snarls, leaping up on the mattress. "You're looking for that idiotic malfeasance? You want to leave with him?! How dare you!" His voice builds to an angry, indignant roar, and the room reflects the god's wrath, floating lights turning scarlet and brightening until the whole room is cast in an angry red light.

The bodies stir, Bacchus' rage rousing from their peaceful, sexed-out slumber.

"What's going on?" Dahlia moans, one twiggy hand scrubbing away bark that had grown over her eyes.

"Our lord is clearly vexed," Eryth growls, untangling her scaly body from a pair of minotaurs. Her angry yellow gaze fixates on me. "Why is he vexed, Delilah?"

I shake my head and shrug my shoulders. "I don't know, because he's a raging fucking narcissist?" I turn back to Bacchus and raise an eyebrow. "What the fuck is wrong with you?"

"Wrong with me?" Bacchus sneers. "Wrong with me?! The fact you prefer that lesser excuse of a god to me indicates that you're the one who's fucking wrong! For I am Zagreus – son to Persephone, Zeus, and Hades – the chosen heir to Olympus."

"Torn apart by the Titans, remade by Zeus inside Semele," the crowd intones, standing up in unison around me. My instincts have me up on my feet as well, screaming of the danger closing in, and I spin around, looking for the exit. "The dying and undying one, made flesh by the seeds of his fathers and blood of his mothers. He is greatness and light and ecstasy."

"Who the hell are you?" Bacchus asks, grabbing me by my shoulders and shaking. "Where do you get off thinking you can ever do better than – "

The shaking only makes the violent rumble in my stomach intensify, and before he can even finish, I retch. Vomit sprays from my mouth onto his feet and legs in a wet splatter.

The room goes silent as Bacchus' mouth falls open in shock, all eyes falling to the mess I've made of his shoes. I quickly wipe my mouth with the back of my hand, head pounding from the rapidly escalating series of events.

"Are you… Did you… *Ugh*!" he pushes me away from him a second later and stares at his feet. "This is fucking disgusting. Dahlia, Eryth attend to me. Everyone else… rip her apart! If she won't be mine, I'll be damned if I'll let anyone else have her."

Dahlia and Eryth quickly rush to his side, but I'm too distracted by the crowd slowly pushing in around me, their eyes dark and filled with madness. I back away, skin vibrating with alarm, searching for an opening.

Mona Ventress

"The one who does it will get the privilege of being the first Maenad to return to service in my entourage," Bacchus adds.

My heart stops in my chest. Alyxs mentioned last night that everyone in the club had been former Maenads – all pushed out like she's about to be. Given her reaction...

"Okay, Hermes," I mutter nervously under my breath. "Now's the time for you to come get me out of here." He doesn't respond, or if he does, it's lost as the crowd surges toward me, an avalanche of inhuman bodies coming directly for me.

Somehow, I find the good sense to run, scrambling through an opening between a pair of legs, and following it to an open pocket of space which I dart through. Appendages reach for me, searching for grips on my arms, shoulders, and legs, but they all glance off, leaving only angry scrapes in their wake. I zig-zag through the crowd, searching for a way out.

Something hulking looms up in front of me, forcing me to stop, and I gape as a series of boulders come together in the vague shape of a ten-foot-tall man. It reaches for me, and I backpedal, scrambling just out of range as the tinier rocks in its 'hand' come together with a *clack*.

My heel catches on something and I lose my balance. Arms whirling, I fight to maintain my footing, but my momentum is too great, and the floor races up to meet my face. My body instinctively curls for the impact.

Something wraps around my legs and stomach, catching me before I can hit.

Looking down, my eyes go wide at the mass of tentacles entangling my legs, and I smile, remembering last night and that moment with Alyxs. I glance back, certain the Maenad already has an escape plan in mind. Instead, her black eyes are hooded and brimming with desperation.

Crap. She's still fighting for a place at his side. "Don't do this," I shout, kicking my legs in a pathetic attempt to free myself from her. "You can't do this!"

"It's my only chance," she retorts helplessly, shaking her head. "It's the only chance I have to keep him!"

Tentacles that had been the source of intense pleasure just hours ago shoot up higher around my limbs and pulls. I resist, but I have all the strength of a paper doll compared to her form and can feel my joints beginning to pop.

"Alyxs, please," I beseech, meeting her gaze and holding it. "Please! I know you're hooked on this essence or wine or whatever magical dick juice he's got going on, but you know this isn't good for you! You know he isn't good for you, that he's using you. You deserve so much better than this! Than him!"

The tension in her muscles falters, her face going slack. She looks past my shoulder, eyeing the crowd rapidly surrounding us and hesitates. "I…"

Yes, I think, confidence blossoming. *I've reached*

her!

Suddenly, a shadow looms up behind her. There's a sharp crack. Suddenly, we're both falling.

I barely realize someone's hit her before something's grabbing me roughly around the waist and jerking me into the air. I scream and kick, not wanting to die, when a masculine voice shouts, "Hermes sent me!" Opening my eyes, I find myself in the arms of a tall man, holding me at least a foot over the crowd. He swings me around in ways that make my stomach lurch, and suddenly I'm astride a horse, clinging to his muscular back with golden blonde hair flowing into my face.

The horse flexes between my thighs, and we spring into a gallop, barreling past all sorts of creatures. I wrap my arms around my savior and clench my eyelids tight, knowing I can either watch and risk throwing up again, or let my rescuer do his thing and vomit later.

"Stop them," Bacchus roars behind us, and I hear what sounds like hundreds of feet barreling toward us from every direction. Muscles pump under us as the horse picks up speed, and I tighten my legs to keep from falling.

For several seconds, there is nothing but the sound of us running, hooves and feet making a rolling thunder that I can feel in my spine. Then something electric races over my skin, and the entire atmosphere changes, signaled by a warm air carrying the scent of damp soil filling my nostrils. Bright light filters through my eyelids, and against my better judgment, I open my eyes.

Yellow sunlight glares down overhead, warming a golden field of tall, yellow reeds that shift and move in the breeze like waves on the ocean. Mountains jut up from the earth in the distance, looming up ominously as the sun begins its descent toward them. Between us and the mountains stands a forest, one that stretches out in every direction as far as I can see.

Glancing over my shoulder, I see a black door frame standing upright in the center of the field, and even though there is nothing but blue skies around it, the interior is dark, with red flashing lights signaling danger.

"Where are we?" I ask.

My savior twists his head over his shoulder, revealing a thick square jaw covered with stubble and a flat squat nose. "Not out of the woods yet," he informs. He takes a moment to think, then adds. "Or rather, not into them." He laughs at his own joke, revealing a mouth full of white square teeth slightly too big for his mouth.

I blink, not sure I get the joke, and after a second, he shrugs and twists back around, looking at the trail ahead. Beneath us the horse breaks out in a jarring, jolting trot, carrying us toward the distant forest at a pace that makes my stomach resume its angry churn.

Closing my eyes, I focus on my breathing to keep the nausea away but can't help wondering who this man is and why Hermes sent him instead of coming himself.

Author's Note

Thank you so much for getting a little Buzzed on Bacchus with me! When I originally envisioned this project, I always knew that one of my books would have to be devoted to the god of wine. I'm sure a lot of you are wondering why I decided to go with his Roman name instead of the much more popular Greek one, and the truth is: I've got a different plan for my 'D' (ba-dum dsh).

I know, I know; Dionysus is ancient, the original seed of darkness in the heart of man, feeding off their drunken states, enticing them to debauchery, driving them to madness. And you're right - in the grand scheme of things - it might have been better to save Dionysis for 'D' and use 'B' for someone else. But I have a plan, (an evil plan), and my only hope is you'll hang on and wait for my vision to unfurl before deciding if this was a good move or not. Also, I kinda wanted to push Delilah into the deep end of this exchange and really challenge her, and who better to subvert expectations than Bacchus?

All that said, I hope you're as excited as I am to explore the next chapter in Delilah's tale, Capturing Centaurs. My goal is to get it to you by August 15th, 2022, but there's been a few big changes early on this year that I'm still adjusting to, and while it means considerably less stress for me overall, I'm still trying to get back into the rhythm of writing. I'll keep you updated on my progress through my social media and feel free to support me through Patreon, as incentivization to get me to work.

Mona Ventress

Lastly, thanks so much for coming with me on this journey. I can't tell you how much I love the premise of the series, and hope I can do it justice, but ever since its conception, I knew it had the potential to be something special. I'm glad you think so too.

Mwuah,

Mona

Works by Mona Ventress

Lover of Mythic Proportions:

Anointed by Anubis

Buzzed on Bacchus

Future Titles:

Capturing Centaurs

Diddlin' the Dryad

Made in the USA
Monee, IL
17 May 2022